THE ADVENTURES OF TOM SAWYER

A Kaplan Vocabulary-Building Classic for Young Readers

**Look for more
Kaplan Vocabulary-Building Classics
for Young Readers**

Great Expectations
by Charles Dickens

Treasure Island
by Robert Louis Stevenson

Little Women
by Louisa May Alcott

THE ADVENTURES OF TOM SAWYER

A Kaplan Vocabulary-Building Classic for Young Readers

MARK TWAIN

ABRIDGED

SIMON & SCHUSTER

NEW YORK   LONDON   SYDNEY   TORONTO

Kaplan Publishing
Published by SIMON & SCHUSTER
1230 Avenue of the Americas
New York, NY 10020

Editorial Director: Jennifer Farthing
Project Editor: Sheryl Gordon
Content Manager: Patrick Kennedy
Abridgement and Adaptation: Caroline Leavitt for Ivy Gate Books
Interior Design: Ismail Soyugenc for Ivy Gate Books
Cover Design: Mark Weaver

Manufactured in the United States of America
Published simultaneously in Canada

10 9 8 7 6 5 4 3 2 1

April 2006
ISBN-13: 978-0-7432-6652-9
ISBN-10:   0-7432-6652-8

For information regarding special discounts for bulk purchases,
please contact Simon & Schuster Special Sales at 1-800-456-6798 or
business@simonandschuster.com.

TABLE OF CONTENTS

HOW TO USE THIS BOOK

Mark Twain's *The Adventures of Tom Sawyer* is a classic tale of life in a small town during the early part of the 1800s. Over the years, the exploits of its characters – from the adventure-loving Tom to flirtatious Becky Thatcher to the young outlaw Huckleberry Finn – have entranced thousands of young people. But the book also is a way for young people today to raise their vocabularies – for tests as well as for daily writing and speaking.

Kaplan makes it as easy as 1-2-3 for you to learn dozens – even hundreds – of new words just by reading this classic story. On the right-hand pages you will find the words of Twain's famous novel. On each page you will find words that have been bolded (put into heavy, dark type). These are words you may be tested on, both in your specific subjects and in standardized tests. On the left-hand pages you'll find information about those words: how to pronounce them, what part of speech they are, what they mean, and even synonyms. In short, you'll find everything you will need to master each of these special words in the story.

Not all of the challenging or unusual words in *Tom Sawyer* are likely to be found on tests. Some are words that were used often in Twain's day, 150 years ago and more, but are uncommon today. Others are words that are specific to people's nineteenth-century occupations or activities. Still others were part of the character's dialect, a speech with which Twain was familiar from his own life. You might want to learn these words as well, even though they are not likely to be tested. For this reason we have underlined them and put information about them in the glossary at the back of this book.

You'll also find other helpful features in this book. "Mark Twain" provides useful informa-tion about Twain's life and his books, which will help you enjoy your reading even more. The back of the book also contains a helpful section that will assist you in writing a book report about *Tom Sawyer.* Use it as an organizer to develop and order your thoughts about the book. At the back of the book you will also find discussion questions. These will get you thinking about the characters, events, and meaning of this classic novel. They will also help you get ready to discuss it in class, with friends, or with your family members.

Now that you have found out what is in the book – and how to use it – you can get started reading and enjoying one of the most famous classics of all time.

MARK TWAIN

Mark Twain was born with the name Samuel Langhorne Clemens, in 1835. When he was four years old, the family moved to Hannibal, Missouri, which became the setting for several of the writer's works.

His father died when Clemens was 12, and he soon after left school and went to work to learn the printing trade. He showed an aptitude for writing and soon was writing for a local newspaper. Clemens's adventurous nature, however, led him down other avenues. Beginning at the age of 18, he embarked on a wide range of activities, from river pilot on Mississippi steamboats to a soldier in the Confederate army to a newspaper writer during the Nevada Gold Rush.

By the 1860s, Twain's writings had begun to get attention, and his career was launched. During the next 30 years he wrote a number of remarkable books, including *The Adventures of Tom Sawyer* (1876), *The Adventures of Huckleberry Finn* (1884), and *A Connecticut Yankee in King Arthur's Court* (1889).

THE ADVENTURES OF TOM SAWYER

SPECTACLES (<u>spek</u> tuh kuhlz) *n.*
objects used to better one's sight
Synonyms: eyeglasses, glasses

SELDOM (<u>sel</u> duhm) *adv.*
not happening often
Synonyms: rarely, infrequently

CHAPTER 1

"Tom!"

No answer.

"Toм!"

No answer.

"What's with that boy, I wonder? You TOM!"

No answer.

The old lady pulled her **spectacles** down and looked over them about the room. Then she put them up and looked out under them. She **seldom** or never looked *through* them for so small a thing as a boy. They were her fancy pair, the pride of her

PERPLEXED (per <u>pleksd</u>) *adj.*
troubled with uncertainty or doubt
Synonyms: confused, discouraged

CONSTITUTE (<u>kon</u> stuh toot) *v.* **-ing**, **-ed**
to be the parts that make up a whole
Synonyms: compose, comprise, form

CALCULATE (<u>kal</u> kyuh late) *v.* **-ing**, **-ed**
to figure out
Synonyms: compute, figure

ARREST (uh <u>rest</u>) *v.* **-ing**, **-ed**
to hold, to seize
Synonyms: halt, stop

heart and were built for "style," not service. She could have seen through a pair of stove-lids just as well. She looked **perplexed** for a moment and then said, not fiercely, but still loud enough for the furniture to hear:

"Well, if I get hold of you I'll—"

She did not finish, for by this time she was bending down and searching under the bed with the broom. She returned with nothing but the cat.

"I never did see the beat of that boy!"

She went to the open door and stood in it and looked out among the tomato vines and weeds that **constituted** the garden. No Tom. So she lifted up her voice at an angle that **calculated** the greatest distance and shouted:

"Y-o-u-u *Tom*!"

There was a slight noise behind her and she turned just in time to seize a small boy by the collar and **arrest** his flight.

"There! I might 'a' thought of that closet. What you been doing in there?"

"Nothing."

TORMENT (tor <u>ment</u>) *v.* **-ing, -ed**
to upset someone or irritate them on purpose
Synonyms: aggravate, annoy, torture

CONSCIENCE (<u>kon</u> shuhnss) *n.*
knowledge of wrong or right, that part of a
person that knows wrong from right
Synonym: morality

"Nothing! Look at your hands. And look at your mouth. What *is* that mess?"

"I don't know, aunt."

"Well, I know. It's jam – that's what it is. Forty times I've said if you didn't let that jam alone I'd skin you.

"My! Look behind you, aunt!"

The old lady whirled round and snatched her skirts out of danger. The lad fled on the instant, scrambled up the high fence, and disappeared over it.

His Aunt Polly stood surprised a moment, and then broke into a gentle laugh.

"Hang the boy, can't I never learn anything? Ain't he played me tricks enough like that for me to be looking out for him by this time? He seems to know just how long he can **torment** me before I get mad. He's my own dead sister's boy, poor thing, and I ain't got the heart to lash him. Every time I let him off, my **conscience** does hurt me so, and every time I hit him my old heart almost breaks. He'll play <u>hooky</u> this afternoon. I'll just have to make him work tomorrow to punish him. It's mighty

GUILE (guy ull) *n.*
treacherous cunning, skillful deceit
Synonyms: craftiness, cleverness

CONFESSION (kuhn fess un) *n.*
statement that you have done something
wrong
Synonyms: admission, declaration

SUSPICION (suh spish uhn) *n.*
a thought that something is wrong, bad, or
dangerous
Synonyms: distrust, doubt

hard to make him work Saturdays, when all the boys is having holiday. He hates work more than he hates anything else, and I've *got* to do some of my duty by him, or I'll spoil the child."

Tom did play hooky, and he had a very good time. While Tom was eating his supper, and stealing sugar as chance offered, Aunt Polly asked him questions that were full of **guile**, for she wanted to trap him into damaging **confessions**.

"Tom, it was a little warm in school, wasn't it?"

"Yes'm."

"Powerful warm, wasn't it?"

"Yes'm."

"Didn't you want to go in a-swimming, Tom?"

A bit of a scare shot through Tom – a touch of uncomfortable **suspicion**. He searched Aunt Polly's face, but it told him nothing. So he said:

"No'm – well, not very much."

The old lady reached out her hand and felt Tom's shirt and said:

"But you ain't too warm now, though." And

VANISH (<u>van</u> ish) *v.* **-ing, -ed**
to go out of sight quickly and unexpectedly
Synonym: disappear

SECURELY (si <u>kyoor</u> lee) *adv.*
closed tightly, not likely to fail
Synonyms: firmly, strongly

SAGACITY (suh <u>gass</u> uh tee) *n.*
soundness in judgment or wisdom
Synonyms: intelligence, insight, perception,

OBEDIENT (oh <u>bee</u> dee uhnt) *adj.*
tending to do what people tell you to do
Synonyms: dutiful, compliant

it pleased her to see that she had discovered that the shirt was dry without anybody knowing that that was what she had in her mind. Tom saw what might be the next move.

"Some of us pumped water on our heads – mine's damp yet. See?"

Aunt Polly was cross to think she had missed that bit of evidence. Then she had a new idea:

"Tom, you didn't have to undo your shirt collar where I sewed it, to pump water on your head, did you? Unbutton your jacket!"

The trouble **vanished** out of Tom's face. He opened his jacket. His shirt collar was **securely** sewed.

"Bother! Well, go 'long with you. I was sure you'd played hooky and been a-swimming. But I forgive ye, Tom. *This* time."

She was half sorry her **sagacity** had been misplaced and half glad that Tom was being **obedient** for once.

But Tom's half-brother Sidney said:

"Well, now, if I didn't think you sewed his collar with white thread, but it's black."

SHABBY (<u>shab</u> ee) *adj.*
    run down, needing to be repaired
      Synonyms: scruffy, tattered

ASTOUNDING (uh <u>stown</u> ding) *adj.*
    astonishing or surprising
      Synonyms: shocking, confusing, amazing

DAINTY (<u>dayn</u> tee) *adj.*
    small and not strong or sturdy
      Synonyms: delicate, refined

"Why, I did sew it with white! Tom!"

But Tom did not wait for the rest. As he went out the door he said:

"Siddy, I'll <u>lick</u> you for that."

Within two minutes, or even less, he had forgotten all his troubles. Suddenly, a stranger was before him – a boy a bit larger than himself. A newcomer of any age or either sex was a curiosity in the poor little **shabby** village of St. Petersburg. This boy was well dressed, too well dressed on a week-day. This was simply **astounding**. His cap was a **dainty** thing, and his clothes were new. He had shoes on – and it was only Friday. The more Tom stared at the boy, the higher the boy turned up his nose and the shabbier and shabbier Tom's own outfit seemed to Tom to grow. Neither boy spoke. If one moved, the other moved – but only sidewise, in a circle. They kept face to face and eye to eye all the time. Finally Tom said:

"I can lick you!"

"I'd like to see you try it."

"Well, I can do it."

"No, you can't, either."

GLOWER (<u>glow</u> ur) *v.* **-ing, -ed**
    to show ill humor, to wear a dark scowl
        Synonyms: glare, frown

ADVANTAGE (ad <u>van</u> tij) *n.*
    something that can give you the upper hand or
    an edge
        Synonyms: benefit, help

PROMPTLY (<u>prompt</u> lee) *adv.*
    quickly, done without delay
        Synonyms: swiftly, rapidly, punctually

DERISION (der <u>izh</u> uhn) *n.*
    angry scorn
        Synonym: disrespect

"Aw – take a walk!"

"Say – if you give me much more of your <u>sass</u> I'll take and bounce a rock off'n your head."

"Oh, of *course* you will."

"Well, I *will*."

Presently they were shoulder to shoulder. Tom said:

"Get away from here!"

"Go away yourself!"

"I won't."

"*I* won't either."

So they stood, each with a foot placed at an angle, both shoving and **glowering** at each other with hate. But neither could get an **advantage**.

Tom drew a line in the dust with his big toe, and said:

"I dare you to step over that, and I'll fight you till you can't stand up."

The new boy stepped over **promptly**, and said:

"You said you'd do it, now let's see you do it."

"For two cents I *will* do it."

The new boy took coins out of his pocket and held them out with **derision**. Tom struck them to

PRESENTLY (<u>prez</u> uhnt lee) *adv.*
happening at that particular time
Synonyms: currently, now

SMOTHERED (smuth <u>urd</u>) *adj.*
thickly covered or coated by something
Synonyms: suffocated, stifled, choked

AMBUSH (ahm <u>buss</u> skade) *n.*
a surprise attack, something that comes
without warning
Synonym: trap

ADAMANTINE (<u>add</u> uh man teen) *adj.*
unyielding, inflexible
Synonyms: tough, unchanging, unbreakable

the ground. In an instant both boys were rolling and tumbling in the dirt, gripped together like cats. For the space of a minute they tugged and tore at each other's hair and clothes and covered themselves with dust. **Presently** the confusion took form, and through the fog of battle Tom appeared, pounding the new boy with his fists. "Holler 'nuff!" said he.

The boy only struggled to free himself.

"Holler 'nuff!" – and the pounding went on.

At last the stranger got out a **smothered** "'Nuff!" and Tom let him up and said:

"Now that'll learn you. Better look out who you're fooling with next time."

He got home pretty late that night, and when he climbed carefully in at the window, he uncovered an **ambush**, in the person of his aunt. When she saw the state his clothes were in, her decision to turn his Saturday holiday into hard labor became **adamantine** in its firmness.

ISSUE (<u>ish</u> oo) *v.* **-ing**, **-ed**
　to send out or give
　　Synonyms: follow, come out

REPOSEFUL (ruh <u>pose</u> full) *adj.*
　free from activity
　　Synonyms: calm, restful

MELANCHOLY (<u>mel</u> uhn kol ee) *n.*
　the state of feeling sad and unwell
　　Synonyms: sadness, depression

CHAPTER 2

Saturday morning came, and all the summer world was bright and fresh. There was a song in every heart. And if the heart was young music **issued** at the lips. Everything was dreamy, **reposeful**, and inviting.

Tom appeared on the sidewalk with a bucket of white paint and a long-handled brush. He looked at the fence, and all gladness left him, and a deep **melancholy** settled down upon his spirit. Thirty yards of board-fence nine feet high. Sighing, he dipped his brush and passed it along the

OPERATION (op uh <u>ray</u> shuhn) *n.*
   a planned event or action
      Synonyms: procedure, process

DISCOURAGED (diss <u>kur</u> ijd) *adj.*
   lacking in enthusiasm or confidence
      Synonyms: dispirited, disheartened

EXCHANGE (eks <u>chaynj</u>) *n.*
   a trade off, a giving of one thing and getting of
   something else
      Synonyms: swap, switch, barter

INSPIRATION (in spihr <u>ay</u> shuhn) *n.*
   something that fills you with emotion or
   passion
      Synonym: brainstorm

SLACKEN (<u>slak</u> uhn) *v.* **-ing**, **-ed**
   to loosen, to allow more freedom
      Synonyms: relax, calm

top most plank, repeated the **operation**, did it again, compared the small whitewashed streak with the far-reaching mass of unwhitewashed fence, and sat down on a tree-box, **discouraged**.

He began to think of the fun he had planned for this day, and his sadness grew. He got out his worldly wealth and examined it – bits of toys, marbles, and trash. It was enough to buy an **exchange** of *work,* maybe, but not half enough to buy so much as half an hour of pure freedom. He gave up the idea of trying to get someone else to do the work. At this dark and hopeless moment an **inspiration** burst upon him!

He took up his brush and went calmly to work. Ben Rogers came in sight – the very boy, of all boys, whose opinion he feared. Ben's walk was a hop-skip-and-jump – proof enough that his heart was light and his hopes, high. He was eating an apple and giving a long, musical whoop, followed by a deep-toned *ding-dong-dong, ding-dong-dong.* He was imitating a steamboat! As he drew near, he **slackened** speed, took the middle of the street, and leaned far over to the

ENVISION (en <u>vih</u> zuhn) *v.* **-ing**, **-ed**
to see in one's mind
Synonyms: observe, foresee, imagine

SURVEY (<u>sur</u> vay) *v.* **-ing**, **-ed**
to look at an entire scene or area
Synonyms: observe, scan

CONTEMPLATE (<u>kon</u> tuhm plate) *v.* **-ing**, **-ed**
to consider carefully and thoughtfully
Synonyms: study, ponder, reflect

left. He was imitating the *Big Missouri* and was everything – boat and captain and engine-bells. So he had to **envision** himself standing on his own hurricane-deck, giving the orders and taking them.

Tom went on whitewashing, paying no attention to the steamboat. Ben stared a moment and then said: "Hi-Yi! *You're* up a stump, ain't you!"

No answer. Tom **surveyed** his last touch with the eye of an artist, then he gave his brush another gentle sweep and looked at the result, as before. Ben came up alongside of him. Tom's mouth watered for the apple, but he stuck to his work. Ben said:

"Hello, old chap, you got to work, hey?"

Tom turned suddenly and said:

"Why, it's you, Ben! I warn't noticing."

"Say, I'm going in a-swimming, I am. Don't you wish you could? But of course you'd <u>druther work</u>, wouldn't you? Course you would!"

Tom **contemplated** the boy a bit, and said:

"What do you call work?"

"Why, ain't *that* work?"

ABSORBED (ab <u>zorbd</u>) *adj.*
lost in something, taken in, giving one's
complete attention to something
Synonyms: engrossed, immersed

PARTICULAR (pur <u>tik</u> yuh lur) *adj.*
concerned about small detail
Synonyms: careful, exacting, meticulous,
scrupulous

Tom continued his whitewashing and answered carelessly:

"Well, maybe it is, and maybe it ain't. All I know is, it suits Tom Sawyer."

"Oh come, now, you don't mean to let on that you *like* it?"

The brush continued to move.

"Like it? Well, I don't see why I oughtn't to like it. Does a boy get a chance to whitewash a fence every day?"

That put the thing in a new light. Ben stopped eating his apple. Tom swept his brush back and forth, stepped back to note the effect, added a touch here and there, and criticized the effect again. Meanwhile, Ben was watching every move and getting more and more interested, more and more **absorbed**. Presently he said:

"Say, Tom, let *me* whitewash a little."

Tom considered and was about to give in. But he changed his mind. "No – no – I reckon it wouldn't hardly do, Ben," he said solemnly. "You see, Aunt Polly's awful **particular** about this fence. It's right here on the street, you know.

RELUCTANCE (ri <u>luhk</u> tens) *n.*
unwillingness to do something
　Synonym: resistance

ALACRITY (uh <u>lack</u> re tee) *n.*
cheerful readiness, quickness
　Synonyms: enthusiasm, eagerness

SLAUGHTER (<u>slaw</u> tur) *n.*
the destruction or killing of a large number
of things
　Synonym: massacre

Yes, she's *awful* particular about this fence. It's got to be done very careful. I reckon there ain't one boy in a thousand, maybe two thousand, that can do it the way it's got to be done."

"No, is that so? Oh come, now, lemme just try, only just a little. I'd let *you*, if you was me, Tom."

"Ben, I'd like to, honest. But Aunt Polly, well, Jim wanted to do it, but she wouldn't let him. Sid wanted to do it, and she wouldn't let Sid. Now don't you see how I'm fixed? If you was to tackle this fence and anything was to happen to it— "

"Oh, shucks, I'll be just as careful. Now lemme try. Say, I'll give you the core of my apple."

"Well, here. No, Ben, now don't. I'm afeard— "

"I'll give you *all* of it!"

Tom gave up the brush with **reluctance** in his face but **alacrity** in his heart. And while the late steamer *Big Missouri* worked and sweated in the sun, the retired artist sat on a barrel in the shade close by. He dangled his legs, munched his apple, and planned the **slaughter** of more innocents.

JEER (jihr) *v.* **-ing**, **-ed**
to tease someone loudly and meanly
Synonyms: heckle, taunt, mock

DECANTER (di <u>kan</u> tur) *n.*
a fancy bottle with a stopper, a jar that holds liquid
Synonyms: carafe, flask

DILAPIDATED (duh <u>lap</u> uh day tid) *adj.*
crumbling and collapsing, falling down or apart
Synonyms: decaying, rundown

There was no lack of material. Boys happened along every little while. They came to **jeer** but remained to whitewash. By the time Ben was tired, Tom had traded the next chance to Billy Fisher for a kite in good repair. When Billy <u>played out</u>, Johnny Miller bought in for a dead rat and a string to swing it with, and so on, and so on, hour after hour. And when the middle of the afternoon came, from being a boy stuck in poverty that he was in the morning, Tom was literally rolling in wealth. He had, besides the things before mentioned, twelve marbles, and part of a <u>harp</u>. There was also a piece of blue bottle-glass to look through, a key that wouldn't unlock anything, a piece of chalk, and a glass stopper of a **decanter**. He got a tin soldier, a couple of tadpoles, six firecrackers, a kitten with only one eye, a brass doorknob, a dog-collar – but no dog – the handle of a knife, four pieces of orange-peel, and a **dilapidated** old window sash.

He had had a nice, good, idle time all the while – and plenty of company – and the fence had three coats of whitewash on it! If he hadn't run

ATTAIN (uh <u>tayn</u>) *v.* **-ing, -ed**
to achieve, obtain
Synonyms: gain, get, accomplish

CONSIST (kun <u>sisst</u>) *v.* **-ing, -ed**
to be made up of
Synonyms: comprise, construct

OBLIGE (uh <u>blije</u>) *adj.*
to be forced to do something
Synonyms: compelled, required

CONSIDERABLE (kuhn <u>sid</u> uh ruh buhl) *adj.*
a large amount of something
Synonyms: substantial, extensive

CIRCUMSTANCE (<u>sur</u> kuhm stanss) *n.*
the conditions related to an event or action
Synonym: situation

out of whitewash he would have taken the belongings of every boy in the village.

Tom said to himself that it was not such a hollow world, after all. He had discovered a great law of human action without knowing it. Namely, that in order to make a man or a boy want a thing it is only necessary to make the thing difficult to **attain**. Work, he learned, **consists** of whatever a body is *obliged* to do, and play consists of whatever a body is not obliged to do. And this would help him to understand why making fake flowers or slaving at a mill is work, while bowling and climbing <u>Mont</u> <u>Blanc</u> is only fun. There are wealthy gentlemen in England who drive four-horse passenger-coaches twenty or thirty miles on a daily line, in the summer, because the right costs them **considerable** amounts money. But if they were offered wages for the service that would turn it into work, and then they would quit.

The boy thought awhile over the huge change which had taken place in his worldly **circumstances** and then walked toward head-quarters to report.

SOPORIFIC (sop o <u>rif</u> ik) *adj.*
    causing sleep or drowsiness
        Synonyms: hypnotic, calming, numbing,
        tranquilizing

DESERT (di <u>zurt</u>) *v.* **-ing**, **-ed**
    to run away or leave something
        Synonyms: abandon, forsake

CHAPTER 3

Tom presented himself before Aunt Polly, who was sitting by an open window in a pleasant room, which was bedroom, breakfast-room, dining-room, and library combined. The warm summer air, the restful quiet, the smell of the flowers, and the **soporific** murmur of the bees had had their effect. She was nodding' over her knitting. Her spectacles were propped up on her gray head for safety. She had thought that, of course, Tom had **deserted** long ago, and she wondered at seeing him place himself in her

EVIDENCE (<u>ev</u> uh duhnss) *n.*
something that helps prove or bring out
the truth
Synonyms: proof, support, verification

ELABORATELY (i <u>lab</u> ur it lee) *adv.*
in a complicated or careful way
Synonyms: ornately, richly, intricately

DILUTE (duh <u>lute</u>) *v.* **-ing**, **-ed**
to make weaker by adding another substance
Synonyms: weaken, thin

SPLENDOR (<u>splen</u> dur) *n.*
intense, amazing beauty
Synonyms: brilliance, magnificence,
radiance

ACHIEVEMENT (uh <u>cheev</u> muhnt) *n.*
something done successfully
Synonyms: attainment, feat,
accomplishment

power again in this huge way. He said: "Mayn't I go and play now, aunt?"

"What, a'ready? How much have you done?"

"It's all done, aunt."

"Tom, don't lie to me – I can't bear it."

"I ain't, aunt; it IS all done."

Aunt Polly placed small trust in such **evidence**. She went out to see for herself. She would have been happy to find twenty percent of Tom's statement true. When she found the entire fence whitewashed and **elaborately** coated and recoated and even a streak added to the ground, her surprise was almost unspeakable. She said:

"Well, I never! There's no getting round it, you can work when you're a mind to, Tom." And then she **diluted** the compliment by adding, "But it's powerful seldom you're a mind to, I'm bound to say. Well, go 'long and play. But mind you get back some time in a week, or I'll tan you."

She was so overcome by the **splendor** of his **achievement** that she took him into the closet and selected a choice apple and delivered it to him. Then he skipped out.

HASTEN (<u>hayss</u> uhn) *v.* **-ing**, **-ed**
    to move or act quickly
        Synonyms: hurry, rush, speed

CONFLICT (<u>kon</u> flict) *n.*
    an instance of fighting
        Synonyms: battle, disagreement, quarrel

CONDESCEND (kon di <u>send</u>) *v.* **-ing**, **-ed**
    to act as if in a rank below one's self
        Synonym: lower

EMINENCE (<u>em</u> uh nuhns) *n.*
    high ground
        Synonyms: elevation, hill, knoll

APPOINT (uh <u>point</u>) *v.* **-ing**, **-ed**
    to officially assign something
        Synonyms: decide, designate, select

EMBROIDER (em <u>broi</u> durd) *v.* **-ing**, **-ed**
    to sew with a design
        Synonyms: embellish, adorn, decorate

Tom walked around the block and came round into a muddy alley. He presently got safely beyond the reach of punishment and **hastened** toward the public square of the village. There two "military" companies of boys had met for **conflict**, according to previous meeting. Tom was general of one of these armies, and his friend Joe Harper was general of the other. These two great commanders did not **condescend** to fight in person – that being better suited to the still smaller fry – but sat together on an **eminence** and oversaw the field operations by orders delivered through aides.

Tom's army won a great victory after a long and hard-fought battle. Then the dead were counted, prisoners exchanged, the day and terms of the next conflict **appointed**. After this the armies fell into line and marched away, and Tom turned homeward alone.

As he was passing by the house where Jeff Thatcher lived, he saw a girl in the garden – a lovely little blue-eyed creature with yellow hair, white summer shirt, and **embroidered** skirt. The fresh-crowned hero fell without firing a shot. A

VANISH (<u>van</u> ish) *v.* **-ing**, **-ed**
to disappear
Synonyms: leave, evaporate, dissolve

PASSION (<u>pash</u> uhn) *n.*
strong desire or devotion
Synonyms: obsession, infatuation

ADORATION (a duh <u>ray</u> shuhn) *n.*
an intense love or esteem
Synonyms: adulation, esteem

GRIEVE (<u>greev</u>) *v.* **-ing**, **-ed**
to feel sad, usually as result of death
Synonyms: mourn, lament, suffer

THRESHOLD (<u>thresh</u> ohld) *n.*
wood or stone on the floor of a doorway
Synonyms: entrance, doorstep, sill

certain Amy Lawrence **vanished** out of his heart and left not even a memory of herself behind. He had thought he loved her. He had viewed his **passion** as **adoration**. He had been months winning her, and, in one instant of time she had gone out of his heart like a stranger whose visit is done.

He worshipped this new angel with watchful eye till he saw that she had discovered him. Then he pretended he did not know she was there and began to "show off" in all sorts of funny boyish ways, in order to win her attention. He kept up this foolishness for some time. But by-and-by, while he was doing some dangerous gymnastic moves, he looked aside and saw that the little girl was winding her way toward the house. Tom came up to the fence and leaned on it, **grieving** and hoping she would wait awhile longer. She stopped a moment on the steps and then moved toward the door. Tom sighed as she put her foot on the **threshold**. But his face lit up right away, for she tossed a flower over the fence a moment before she disappeared.

The boy ran around and stopped within a foot or two of the flower. Then he shaded his eyes

EXHIBIT (eg <u>zib</u> it) *v.* **-ing, -ed**
to show something publicly
Synonyms: display, reveal, show

RELUCTANTLY (ri <u>luhk</u> tant lee) *adv.*
in a way that is without enthusiasm, not eager
Synonyms: unenthusiastically, unwillingly,
grudgingly, hesitantly

VISION (<u>vizh</u> uhn) *n.*
something imagined or dreamed about
Synonyms: dream, hallucination, fantasy

with his hand and began to look down street as if he had discovered something of interest going on in that direction. Presently he picked up a straw and began trying to balance it on his nose with his head tilted far back. As he moved from side to side, in his efforts, he edged nearer and nearer toward the flower. Finally his bare foot rested upon it, his toes closed upon it, and he hopped away with the treasure and disappeared around the corner.

He returned, now, and hung about the fence till nightfall, "showing off" as before. But the girl never **exhibited** herself again, though Tom comforted himself a little with the hope that she had been near some window, meantime, and had been aware of his attentions. Finally he walked home, **reluctantly**, with his poor head full of **visions**.

All through supper his spirits were so high that his aunt wondered "what had got into the child." He took a good scolding about hitting Sid and did not seem to mind it in the least. He tried to steal sugar under his aunt's very nose and got his knuckles hit for it. He said:

"Aunt, you don't whack Sid when he takes it."

TORMENT (tor <u>ment</u>) *v.* **-ing**, **-ed**
to annoy or upset someone intentionally
Synonyms: antagonize, abuse, harass

IMMUNITY (i <u>myoon</u> uh tee) *n.*
protection from a disease or action
Synonyms: exemption, privilege

UNBEARABLE (uhn <u>bair</u> uh buhl) *adj.*
so bad or unpleasant that one cannot stand it
Synonyms: intolerable, excruciating,
unendurable

EXULTATION (ek suhl <u>tay</u> shuhn) *n.*
an extreme joy or happiness
Synonyms: jubilation, enthusiasm, rejoicing

"Well, Sid don't **torment** a body the way you do. You'd be always into that sugar if I warn't watching you."

Presently she stepped into the kitchen, and Sid, happy in his **immunity**, reached for the sugar bowl – a sort of power over Tom which was **unbearable**. But Sid's fingers slipped, and the bowl dropped and broke. Tom was thrilled. He said to himself that he would not speak a word, even when his aunt came in. He would sit perfectly still till she asked who did the mischief. Then he would tell and there would be nothing so good in the world as to see that pet model "catch it." He was so full of **exultation** that he could hardly hold himself when the old lady came back, and the next instant he was laid out on the floor! The palm was uplifted to strike again when Tom cried out:

"Hold on, now, what 'er you belting ME for? Sid broke it!"

Aunt Polly paused, perplexed, and Tom looked for healing pity. But when she got her tongue again, she only said:

"Umf! Well, you didn't get enough hits, I

DISCIPLINE (<u>diss</u> uh plin) *n.*
command over one's behavior
Synonyms: training, regulation

ACCUSTOMED (uh <u>kuss</u> tuhmd) *adj.*
normal; usual
Synonyms: familiar, habituated; acquainted

SEEK (seek) *v.* **-ing, sought**
to search for something
Synonym: look

DESOLATE (<u>dess</u> uh luht) *adj.*
deserted, without other people
Synonyms: isolated, uninhabited

DREARY (<u>drihr</u> ee) *adj.*
miserable, dull
Synonyms: gloomy, depressing

DEVISE (di <u>vize</u>) *v.* **-ing, -ed**
to think up or invent
Synonyms: develop, plan, create

44

reckon. You been into some other mischief when I wasn't around, like enough."

Then her conscience scolded her, and she longed to say something kind and loving. But she judged that this would be taken as a confession that she had been in the wrong and **discipline** didn't allow that. So she kept silence and went about her affairs with a troubled heart. Tom sulked in a corner, and he got up quickly and moved in clouds and darkness out the door.

He wandered far from the **accustomed** haunts of boys and **sought desolate** places that were matched with his spirit. A log raft in the river invited him, and he seated himself on its outer edge and thought about the **dreary** hugeness of the stream. He wished, the while, that he could only be drowned, all at once and unfeeling without undergoing the uncomfortable routine **devised** by nature. Then he thought of his flower. It was all crumpled and droopy, but it mightily increased his happiness. He wondered if she would pit him if she knew? Would she cry and wish that she had a right to put her arms around his neck

AGONY (<u>ag</u> uh nee) *n.*
intense pain or suffering
Synonyms: anguish, pain, torture

PLEASURABLE (<u>plezh</u> ur uh buhl) *adj.*
giving a feeling of enjoyment
Synonyms: enjoyable, pleasing, gratifying, satisfying

CLASP (<u>klasp</u>) *v.* **-ing**, **-ed**
to hold firmly or tightly
Synonyms: grasp, clutch, grip

WILTED (<u>wilt</u> ed) *adj.*
droopy
Synonyms: sagging, withered, bent

and comfort him? Or would she turn coldly away like all the hollow world? This picture brought such an **agony** of **pleasurable** suffering that he worked it over and over again in his mind and set it up in new and different lights till he wore it down. At last he rose up sighing and departed in the darkness.

About half-past nine or ten o'clock he came along the empty street to where the Loved Unknown lived. He paused a moment, but no sound fell upon his listening ear. A candle was casting a dull glow upon the curtain of a second-story window. He climbed the fence and threaded his way through the plants until he stood under that window. He looked up at it long and, with emotion, laid himself down on the ground under it. He turned himself upon his back, **clasped** his hands upon his breast, and held his poor **wilted** flower. And thus he would die – out in the cold world, with no shelter over his homeless head, no friendly hand to wipe the death-damps from his face, no loving face to bend over him when the great agony came. And thus SHE would see him when she looked out upon the glad morning, and oh! would

MARTYR (<u>mar</u> tur) *n.*

someone killed or made to suffer for his or her beliefs

Synonyms: hero, saint

MISSILE (<u>miss</u> uhl) n.

a weapon that is launched or thrown at a target

Synonyms: projectile, rocket, shot

VAGUE (<u>vayg</u>) *adj.*

unclear, not definite

Synonyms: indistinct, blurred

OMISSION (oh <u>mi</u> shuhn) *n.*

the act of leaving something out or not doing something

Synonyms: exclusion, disregard, absence

she drop one little tear upon his poor, lifeless form, would she heave one little sigh to see a bright young life so rudely cut down?

The window went up, a maid-servant's voice interrupted the calm, and a flood of water soaked the **martyr's** remains!

The hero jumped up with a snort. There was a whiz as of a **missile** in the air, mingled with the whisper of a curse and a sound of shivering glass. Then a small, **vague** form went over the fence and shot away in the darkness.

Not long after, as Tom undressed for bed, Sid woke up. But if he had any dim idea of calling him out on his mischief he thought better of it and held his peace, for there was danger in Tom's eye.

Tom turned in without praying, and Sid made note of the **omission**.

PARIAH (puh rye uh) *n.*
someone thrown out by society
Synonyms: outcast, vagrant

FORBIDDEN (fur bid in) *adj.*
not allowed, not fitting into usual and
acceptable standards
Synonyms: unlawful, unacceptable

CHAPTER 4

Monday, Tom came upon the young **pariah** of the village, Huckleberry Finn, son of the town drunk. Huckleberry was hated and feared by all the mothers of the town because he was idle and lawless and bad. Also, because all their children admired him so, delighted in his **forbidden** society, and wished they dared to be like him. Tom was like the rest of the good boys, in that he was jealous of Huckleberry's free condition, and he was under strict orders not to play with him. So he played Huckleberry every time he got a

PERENNIAL (puh <u>ren</u> ee uhl) *adj.*
    active or enduring all through the year
        Synonyms: constant, persistent

DISARRAY (diss uh <u>ray</u>) *n.*
    a lack of order
        Synonyms: disorder, confusion, messiness

VAST (<u>vast</u>) *adj.*
    very great in degree or intensity
        Synonyms: tremendous, huge

HAIL (hayl) *v.* **-ing**, **-ed**
    to call out or say hello to someone
        Synonyms: greet, salute

chance. Huckleberry was always dressed in the cast-off clothes of full-grown men, and they were in **perennial disarray** and fluttering with rags. His hat was a **vast** ruin with a wide moon-shape cut out of its brim. His coat, when he wore one, hung nearly to his heels and had the rearward buttons far down the back. There was only one suspender to support his trousers. The seat of the trousers bagged low and contained nothing, the cut up legs dragged in the dirt when not rolled up.

Tom **hailed** the romantic outcast:

"Hello, Huckleberry!"

"Hello, yourself, and see how you like it."

"What's that you got?"

"Dead cat."

"Lemme see him, Huck. My, he's pretty stiff. Say – where did you get him, Huck?"

"Bought him off a boy."

"What did you give for him?"

"I give a blue steamboat ticket and a pig's ear I got at the slaughterhouse."

"Where'd you get the ticket?"

ISOLATED (<u>eye</u> suh layt ed) *adj.*
kept separate from other things
Synonyms: secluded, withdrawn

BRISKLY (<u>brisk</u> lee) *adv.*
with speed and energy
Synonyms: rapidly, energetically

LULL (luhl) *v.* **-ing**, **-ed**
to make someone feel peaceful or sleepy
Synonym: quiet

REFUGE (<u>ref</u> yooj) *n.*
a place safe from danger or trouble
Synonyms: sanctuary, protection

SYMPATHY (<u>sim</u> puh thee) *n.*
support and agreement
Synonyms: compassion, understanding

"Bought it off'n Ben Rogers for shiny piece of metal I found."

"Say – what are dead cats good for anyway, Huck?"

"Good for? Cure warts with, that's what."

"Hmm, you think so? Well, I best be heading back to school, Huck."

When Tom reached the little **isolated** wooden schoolhouse, he strode in **briskly**, with the manner of one who had come with all honest speed. He hung his hat on a peg and flung himself into his seat with business-like alacrity. The master, throned on high in his great armchair, was sleeping, **lulled** by the hum of study. The interruption woke him.

"Thomas Sawyer!"

Tom knew that when his name was said in full, it meant trouble.

"Come up here. Now, sir, why are you late again, as usual?"

Tom was about to take **refuge** in a lie, when he saw two long tails of yellow hair hanging down a back that he recognized by the electric **sympathy**

ASTOUNDING (uh <u>stound</u> ing) *adj.*
    causing surprise or astonishment
        Synonym: shocking

NOTABLY (<u>noh</u> tuh blee) *adv.*
    to a point that is worthy of notice
        Synonyms: particularly, conspicuously,
    remarkably

RIPPLE (<u>rip</u> uhl) *v.* **-ing, -ed**
    to flow with a slight rise and fall
        Synonym: swell

ABASH (uh <u>bash</u>) *v.* **-ing, -ed**
    to make self-conscious
        Synonyms: embarrass, humiliate, humble

of love. And next to that form was THE ONLY VACANT PLACE on the girls' side of the schoolhouse. He instantly said:

"I STOPPED TO TALK WITH HUCKLE-BERRY FINN!"

The master's pulse stood still, and he stared helplessly. The buzz of study stopped. The pupils wondered if this foolhardy boy had lost his mind. The master said:

"You – you did what?"

"Stopped to talk with Huckleberry Finn."

There was no mistaking the words.

"Thomas Sawyer, this is the most **astounding** confession I have ever listened to. No mere scolding will answer for this offence. Take off your jacket."

The master's arm performed until it was tired and the number of hits upon Tom's backside **notably** slowed. Then the order followed:

"Now, sir, go and sit with the girls! And let this be a warning to you."

The whispering that **rippled** around the room appeared to **abash** the boy. But in reality that result was caused rather more by the worship that

FURTIVE (<u>fur</u> tiv) *adj.*
   taken without permission
      Synonyms: sneaky, sly, secretive

OBSERVE (uhb <u>zurv</u>) *v.* **-ing, -ed**
   to see or watch
      Synonyms: notice, perceive

ANIMOSITY (an uh <u>mawss</u> uh tee) *n.*
   an attitute of hostility
      Synonyms: hatred, loathing

MANIFEST (<u>man</u> uh fest) *v.* **-ing, -ed**
   make evident
      Synonyms: exhibit, display, expose

resulted and the pleasure that lay in his high good fortune. He sat down upon the end of the pine bench and the girl pushed herself away from him with a toss of her head. Nudges and winks and whispers traveled the room, but Tom sat still, with his arms upon the long, low desk before him, and seemed to study his book.

By and by attention left him, and the usual school murmur rose upon the quiet air once more. Presently the boy began to steal **furtive** glances at the girl. She **observed** it, "made a mouth" at him and gave him the back of her head for the space of a minute. When she faced around again, a peach lay before her. She put it aside. Tom gently put it back. She thrust it away again but with less **animosity**. Tom patiently returned it to its place. Then she let it remain. Tom wrote on his <u>slate</u>, "Please take it – I got more."

The girl glanced at the words, but made no sign. Now the boy began to draw something on his slate, hiding his work with his left hand. For a time the girl refused to notice, but her human curiosity presently began to **manifest** itself by

PERCEPTIBLE (pur <u>sep</u> tuh buhl) *adj.*
easily seen or noticeable
Synonyms: clear, detectable

HESITATINGLY (<u>hez</u> uh tay ting lee) *adv.*
doing something with doubt or indecision
Synonyms: reluctantly, timidly

CARICATURE (<u>ka</u> ri kuh chur) *n.*
an embellished drawing of someone or something
Synonyms: imitation, cartoon

HYPERCRITICAL (hye pur <u>krit</u> uh kuhl) *adj.*
overly critical or picky
Synonyms: disapproving, fussy

hardly **perceptible** signs. The boy worked on, unconscious. The girl made a sort of attempt to see, but the boy did not show that he was aware of it. At last she gave in and **hesitatingly** whispered:

"Let me see it."

Tom partly uncovered a **caricature** of a house with two ends to it and a corkscrew of smoke coming from the chimney. Then the girl's interest began to fasten itself upon the work, and she forgot everything else. When it was finished, she looked a moment, then whispered:

"It's nice – make a man."

The artist made a man in the front yard, which looked like a stick figure. He could have stepped over the house, but the girl was not **hypercritical**. She was satisfied with the monster and whispered:

"It's ever so nice – I wish I could draw."

"It's easy," whispered Tom, "I'll learn you."

"Oh, will you? When?"

"At noon. Do you go home to dinner?"

"I'll stay if you will."

"Good – that's a whack. What's your name?"

SCUFFLE (<u>skuhf</u> uhl) *n.*
a confused, disorganized fight
Synonyms: commotion, altercation, tussle

ENSUE (en <u>soo</u>) *v.* **-ing**, **-ed**
to happen as result of something else
Synonyms: result, follow

REVEAL (ri <u>veeld</u>) *v.* **-ing**, **-ed**
made known
Synonyms: told, exposed

JUNCTURE (<u>juhngk</u> chur) *n.*
a turning point
Synonyms: moment, crossroad, occasion

"Becky Thatcher. What's yours? Oh, I know. It's Thomas Sawyer."

"That's the name they lick me by. I'm Tom when I'm good. You call me Tom, will you?"

Now Tom began to draw something on the slate, hiding the words from the girl. But she was not backward this time. She begged to see. Tom said:

"You'll tell."

"No, I won't – no and no and double no, I won't."

"You won't tell anybody at all?"

"No, I won't ever tell ANYbody. Now let me."

"Oh, YOU don't want to see!"

"Now that you treat me so, I WILL see." And she put her small hand upon his and a little **scuffle ensued**. Tom pretended to resist but let his hand slip by degrees till these words **revealed** themselves: "I LOVE YOU."

"Oh, you bad thing!" And she hit his hand a smart smack, but she reddened and looked pleased, nevertheless.

Just at this **juncture**, the boy felt a slow grip

IMPULSE (<u>im</u> puhlss) *n.*

    1. a sudden action

      Synonyms: force, thrust

    2. a sudden desire to take action

      Synonyms: urge, whim, inclination

closing on his ear and a steady lifting **impulse**. In that grip he was thrown across the house and put in his own seat, under a fire of giggles from the whole school. Then the master stood over him during a few awful moments, until he finally moved away to his throne without saying a word. But although Tom's ear tingled, his heart was happy.

BLISS (<u>bliss</u>) *n.*
complete happiness
Synonyms: delight, ecstasy

CHAPTER 5

When they met up again, Tom was swim-
ming in **bliss**. They sat at a table at their very
private school. He said:

Say, Becky, was you ever <u>engaged</u>?"

"What's that?"

"Why, engaged to be married."

"No."

"Would you like to?"

"I reckon so. I don't know. What is it like?"

"Like? Why it ain't like anything. You only
just tell a boy you won't ever have anybody but

TIMIDLY (<u>tim</u> id lee) *adv.*

done without bravery or self-confidence

Synonyms: nervously, shyly, fearfully

SEIZE (<u>seez</u>) *v.* **-ing, -ed**

to take hold of something

Synonyms: grab, snatch, clutch

SUBMIT (suhb <u>mit</u>) *v.* **-ing, -ed**

to give in to someone else's decision

Synonyms: surrender, comply, defer

him, ever ever ever, and then you kiss and that's all. Anybody can do it."

"Kiss? What do you kiss for?"

"Why, that, you know, is to – well, they always do that."

"Everybody?"

"Why, yes, everybody that's in love with each other."

She bent **timidly** around till her breath moved his curls and whispered, "I – love – you!"

Then she sprang away and ran around and around the desks and benches, with Tom after her, and took refuge in a corner at last, her hands holding her little white apron to her face. Tom **seized** her about her neck and pleaded:

"Now, Becky, it's all done – all over but the kiss. Don't you be afraid of that – it ain't anything at all. Please, Becky." And he tugged at her apron and the hands.

By and by she gave up and let her hands drop. Her face, all glowing with the struggle, came up and **submitted**. Tom kissed the red lips and said:

"Now it's all done, Becky. And always after

ASPECT (<u>ass</u> pekt) *n.*
   a part of a certain thing
      Synonyms: feature, portion

BLUNDER (<u>bluhn</u> dur) *n.*
   a stupid error
      Synonym: mistake

this, you know, you ain't ever to love anybody but me, and you ain't ever to marry anybody but me, ever, never, and forever. Will you?"

"No, I'll never love anybody but you, Tom, and I'll never marry anybody but you – and you ain't to ever marry anybody but me, either."

"Certainly. Of course. That's one **aspect** of it. And coming to school or when we're going home, you're to walk with me – when there ain't anybody looking, of course. And you choose me and I choose you at parties because that's the way you do when you're engaged."

"It's so nice. I never heard of it before."

"Oh, it's ever so nice! Why, me and Amy Lawrence— "

The big eyes told Tom his **blunder**, and he stopped, confused.

"Oh, Tom! Then I ain't the first you've ever been engaged to!"

The child began to cry. Tom said:

"Oh, don't cry, Becky, I don't care for her any more."

"Yes, you do, Tom – you know you do."

PLEADINGLY (<u>pleed</u> ing lee) *adv.*
said in a begging, apologetic way
Synonyms: beseechingly, imploringly

VISUALIZE (<u>vizh</u> oo uh lize) *v.* **-ing**, **-ed**
to see something
Synonyms: picture, envision, conceive

Tom tried to put his arm about her neck, but she pushed him away, turned her face to the wall, and went on crying.

Tom's heart hurt him. He went to her and stood a moment, not knowing exactly how to proceed. Then he said hesitatingly:

"Becky, I – I don't care for anybody but you."

No reply – just sobs.

"Becky" – **pleadingly** – "Becky, won't you say something?"

More sobs.

Tom got out his most prized jewel, a brass knob from a door, and passed it around her so that she could **visualize** it, and said:

"Please, Becky, won't you take it?"

She struck it to the floor. Then Tom marched out of the house and over the hills and far away, to return to school no more that day.

SUPERSTITION (soo puhr <u>sti</u> shuhn) *n.*
   a belief or practice resulting from ignorance
      Synonyms: belief, notion

PURSUIT (puhr <u>soot</u>) *n.*
   an attempt to follow someone
      Synonyms: chase, hunt

ELASTIC (i <u>lass</u> tik) *adj.*
   able to be shaped, able to stretch and recover
      Synonyms: adaptable, buoyant, resilient

CHAPTER 6

Tom dodged here and there through lanes until he was well out of the track of returning students. Then he fell into a moody jog. He crossed a small stream two or three times because of a youthful **superstition** that to cross water threw off **pursuit**. Now as to this girl. What had he done? Nothing. He had meant the best in the world, and he been treated like a dog – like a very dog. She would be sorry some day – maybe when it was too late.

But the **elastic** heart of youth will not

COMPRESS (kuhm <u>press</u>) *v.* **-ing**, **- ed**
    to press or squeeze something together
        Synonyms: constrict, cramp, restrict

ECSTASY (<u>ek</u> stuh see) *n.*
    overwhelming joy
        Synonyms: delight, bliss

CAREER (kuh <u>rihr</u>) *n.*
    the work that a person does
        Synonyms: occupation, employment,
    livelihood

ABSENCE (<u>ab</u> suhnss) *n.*
    the state of being missing, not present
        Synonyms: absenteeism, disappearance

CIVILIZATION (siv i luh <u>zay</u> shuhn) *n.*
    a situation of modern life
        Synonyms: society, community

ARRANGEMENT (uh <u>raynj</u> ment) *n.*
    a set program for doing something
        Synonyms: plan, preparation

ACCORDINGLY (uh <u>kord</u> ing lee) *adv.*
    in a way that fits the situation
        Synonyms: suitably, properly

compress into one shape for long. Tom presently began to drift back into the concerns of this life again. He would be a pirate! How his name would fill the world and make people shudder! How gloriously he would go sailing the dancing seas in his long, low, black racer, the *Spirit of the Storm*, with his flag flying at the front! And at the top of his fame, how he would suddenly appear at the old village and walk into church and hear with swelling **ecstasy** the whisperings, "It's Tom Sawyer, the Pirate!"

Yes, it was settled. His **career** was set. He would run away from home and enter upon it.

Tom got the troubles with Becky off his mind by escaping to an island in the middle of the river where he played pirate with Huck and Joe Harper. Their **absence** caused much concern in the town, as many searched unsuccessfully to find them. Feeling guilty about how upset he was making his aunt, Tom convinced the others to return to **civilization** after having disappeared for days. The whole town believed the boys to be dead, and **arrangements** were being made **accordingly**. The

MOURNING (<u>morn</u> ing) *n.*
  a state of grief often accompanied by somber
  dress and various rituals
    Synonyms: bereavement, grieving, sadness

MELANCHOLY (<u>mel</u> uhn kol ee) *adj.*
  sad or depressed
    Synonyms: downhearted, blue, grim

REVERENT (<u>rev</u> ur uhnt) *adj.*
  full of respect and great love
    Synonyms: worshipful, awed

DISPUTE (diss <u>pyoot</u>) *n.*
  a verbal argument
    Synonyms: disagreement, quarrel

DISTINCTION (diss <u>tingk</u> shuhn) *n.*
  something that makes a person or an object
  unusual or different
    Synonyms: feature, mark

Harpers and Aunt Polly's family were going into **mourning**, with great grief and many tears. An unusual quiet came over the village, although it was usually quiet enough, in all conscience.

In the afternoon, Becky Thatcher was feeling very **melancholy**.

She thought:

"Oh, if I only had that brass doorknob again! But I haven't got anything now to remember him by." And she choked back a little sob.

"It was right here. But he's gone now. I'll never, never, never see him any more."

This thought broke her down, and she wandered away with tears rolling down her cheeks. Then quite a group of boys and girls – playmates of Tom's and Joe's – came by and stood looking over the fence, talking in **reverent** tones of how Tom did so-and-so the last time they saw him and how Joe said this and that.

Then there was a **dispute** about who saw the dead boys last in life. Many claimed that sad **distinction** and offered evidences, more or less tampered with by the witness. Finally, it was

ULTIMATELY (<u>uhl</u> tuh mit lee) *adv.*
at last, for the final time
Synonyms: eventually, finally

VESTIBULE (<u>vest</u> uh byool) *n.*
the room or passage between the outer door
and the interior of a building
Synonyms: foyer, lobby, entrance hall

CONSOLE (kuh <u>sole</u>) *v.* **-ing**, **-ed**
to try to make someone feel better about
something
Synonyms: comfort, cheer, encourage

CONGREGATION (kon gri <u>gay</u> shuhn) *n.*
a group of people gathered together, usually for
worship
Synonyms: assembly, parish

RESURRECTION (re zuh <u>rek</u> shuhn) *n.*
the act of returning to life
Synonyms: rebirth, reawakening

ultimately decided who DID see the departed last and exchanged the last words with them. At that point the lucky parties took upon themselves a sort of sacred importance and were gaped at and admired by all the rest.

When the Sunday school hour was finished the next morning, the bell began to <u>toll</u> instead of ringing in the usual way. The villagers began to gather, waiting a moment in the **vestibule** to chat in whispers about the sad event. But there was no whispering in the house, only the rustling of dresses as the women going to their seats disturbed the silence there. There was finally a waiting pause, a waiting dumbness, and then Aunt Polly entered. She was followed by Sid and cousin Mary, who had come to mourn and **console**. They, in turn, were followed by the Harper family, all in black. The whole **congregation**, the old minister as well, rose and stood until the mourners were seated in the front row. There was another silence, broken at times by quiet sobs, and then the minister spread his hands and prayed. A moving song was sung and the text followed: "I am the **Resurrection** and the Life."

INCIDENT (<u>in</u> suh duhnt) *n.*
something that happens
Synonyms: episode, occasion

GENEROUS (<u>jen</u> ur uhss) *adj.*
eager to use time and money to aid others
Synonyms: giving, charitable, unselfish

TRANSFIXED (transs <u>fiksd</u>) *adj.*
without movement
Synonyms: fixed, frozen, paralyzed

As the service went on the clergyman drew verbal pictures of the children. He said he had seen only faults and flaws in the poor boys and had greatly misjudged them. The minister told many a touching **incident** in the lives of the <u>departed</u>, too, which showed their sweet, **generous** natures. The people could easily see, now, how noble and beautiful they were. The congregation became more and more moved as the tale went on, till at last the whole company broke down and joined the weeping mourners in a chorus of sobs, the preacher himself giving way to his feelings and crying in the pulpit.

There was a rustle in the gallery, which nobody noticed. A moment later the church door creaked. The minister raised his streaming eyes above his handkerchief and stood **transfixed**! First one and then another pair of eyes followed the minister's, and then almost with one impulse, the congregation rose and stared while the three dead boys came marching up the aisle: Tom in the lead, Joe next, and Huck, a ruin of drooping rags, sneaking sheepishly in the rear!

ABASHED (uh <u>bashd</u>) *adj.*
seeming to be ashamed
Synonyms: embarrassed, humbled

ABRUPTLY (uh <u>brupt</u> lee) *adv.*
done suddenly and unexpectedly
Synonyms: rapidly, hastily, swiftly

VARYING (<u>vair</u> ee ing) *adj.*
exhibiting change
Synonyms: altering, shifting, fluctuating

They had been hid in the unused gallery listening to their own funeral sermon!

Aunt Polly, Mary, and the Harpers threw themselves upon the children, smothered them with kisses, and poured out thanksgivings, while poor Huck stood **abashed** and uncomfortable, not knowing exactly what to do or where to hide from so many unwelcoming eyes.

Abruptly the minister shouted at the top of his voice: "Praise God from whom all blessings flow – SING! – and put your hearts in it!" And they did.

As the congregation trooped out, Tom got more cuffs and kisses – according to Aunt Polly's **varying** moods – than he had earned before in a year.

FRINGE (frinj) *n.*

a border or an edge

Synonyms: borderline, outskirts

CHAOS (kay oss) *n.*

a confused mass or mixture

Synonyms: confusion, disorder, disarray

CHAPTER 7

That was Tom's great secret – the scheme to return home with his brother pirates and attend their own funerals. They had paddled back over to the Missouri shore on a log at dusk on Saturday, landing five or six miles below the village. They had slept in the woods on the **fringe** of the town till nearly daylight. They had then crept through back lanes and alleys and finished their sleep in the gallery of the church among a **chaos** of natural benches.

At breakfast Monday morning, Aunt Polly

ATTENTIVE (uh <u>ten</u> tiv) *adj.*
paying close attention to the needs of others
Synonyms: considerate, accommodating

and Mary were very loving to Tom and very **attentive** to his wants. There was an unusual amount of talk. In the course of it Aunt Polly said:

"Well, I don't say it wasn't a fine joke, Tom, to keep everybody suffering 'most a week so you boys had a good time. But it is a pity you could be so hard-hearted as to let me suffer so. If you could come over on a log to go to your funeral, you could have come over and give me a hint some way that you warn't dead, but only run off."

"Yes, you could have done that, Tom," said Mary. "And I believe you would if you had thought of it."

"Would you, Tom?" said Aunt Polly.

"Say, now, would you, if you'd thought of it?"

"I – well, I don't know. 'Twould a spoiled everything."

"Tom, I hoped you loved me that much," said Aunt Polly, with a tone that discomforted the boy. "It would have been something if you'd cared enough to THINK of it, even if you didn't DO it."

PLEAD (<u>pleed</u>) *v.* **-ing**, **-ed**
to argue in one's defense
Synonyms: defend, respond

REPENTANT (ri <u>pen</u> tuhnt) *adj.*
expressive of apology
Synonyms: apologetic, regretful, remorseful

"Now, auntie, that ain't any harm," **pleaded** Mary. "It's only Tom's <u>giddy</u> way – he is always in such a rush that he never thinks of anything."

"More's the pity. Sid would have thought. And Sid would have come and DONE it, too. Tom, you'll look back some day, when it's too late, and wish you'd cared a little more for me when it would have cost you so little."

"Now, auntie, you know I do care for you," said Tom.

"I'd know it better if you acted more like it."

"I wish now I'd thought," said Tom, with a **repentant** tone. "But I dreamt about you, anyway. That's something, ain't it?"

"It ain't much – a cat does that much – but it's better than nothing. What did you dream?"

"Why, Wednesday night I dreamt that you was sitting over there by the bed, and Sid was sitting by the woodbox, and Mary next to him."

"Well, so we did. So we always do. I'm glad your dreams could take even that much trouble about us."

"And I dreamt Joe Harper's mother was here."

ALLEGE (uh <u>lej</u>) *v.* **-ing**, **-ed**
to say something is true without proof
Synonyms: state, assert

VIVID (<u>vi</u> vuhd) *adj* .
producing clear mental images
Synonyms: bright, intense, lucid

"Mercy on us! Go on, Tom – go on!"

"And it seems to me that you said, 'Why, I believe that that door—'"

"Go ON, Tom!"

"Just let me study a moment – just a moment. Oh, yes – you said you **alleged** the door was open."

"As I'm sitting here, I did! Didn't I, Mary!"

"And then – and then – well I won't be certain, but it seems as if you made Sid go and – and—"

"Well? Well? What did I make him do, Tom? What did I make him do?"

"You made him – Oh, you made him shut it."

"Well, for the land's sake! I never heard the beat of that in all my days! Don't tell ME there ain't anything in dreams, any more. Sereny Harper shall know of this before I'm an hour older. I'd like to see her get around THIS with her rubbage 'bout superstition. Go on, Tom!"

"Oh, it's all getting just as **vivid** as day, now. Next you said I warn't BAD, only mischievous and harum-scarum, and I warn't any more responsible than – than – I think it was a colt, or something."

"And so it was! Well, goodness! Go on, Tom!"

PROPHESY (<u>pro</u> fuh see) *n.*
a prediction of something to come
Synonyms: forecast, foretelling

"And then you began to cry."

"So I did. So I did. Not the first time, neither. And then—"

"Then Mrs. Harper she began to cry, and said Joe was just the same, and she wished she hadn't whipped him for taking cream when she'd throwed it out her own self—"

"Tom! The sperrit was upon you! You was making **prophesies** – that's what you was doing! Land alive, go on, Tom!"

"Then Sid he said – he said— "

"I don't think I said anything," said Sid.

"Yes you did, Sid," said Mary.

"Shut your heads and let Tom go on! What did he say, Tom?"

"He said – I THINK he said he hoped I was better off where I was gone to, but if I'd been better sometimes— "

"THERE, d'you hear that! It was his very words!"

"And you shut him up sharp."

"I lay I did! There must a been an angel there. There WAS an angel there, somewheres!"

NEFARIOUS (nuh <u>fair</u> ee uhss) *adj.*
full of evil
Synonyms: shameful, wicked

VANQUISH (<u>vang</u> kwish) *v.* **-ing**, **-ed**
to overcome
Synonyms: conquer, defeat, overpower

"And Mrs. Harper told about Joe scaring her with a firecracker, and you told about Peter and the Painkiller— "

"Just as true as I live!"

"Then I thought you prayed for me – and I could see you and hear every word you said. And you went to bed, and I was so sorry that I took and wrote on a piece of tree bark, 'We ain't dead – we are only off being pirates,' and put it on the table by the candle. And then you looked so good, laying there asleep, that I thought I went and leaned over and kissed you on the lips."

"Did you, Tom, DID you! I just forgive you everything for that!" And she seized the boy in a crushing embrace that made him feel like the most **nefarious** of villains.

The children left for school, and the old lady went to call on Mrs. Harper and **vanquish** her sadness with Tom's great dream. Sid had better judgment than to utter the thought that was in his mind as he left the house. It was this: "Pretty thin – as long a dream as that, without any mistakes in it!"

DIGNIFIED (<u>dig</u> nuh fide) *adj.*
distinguished, composed
Synonyms: elegant

ELOQUENT (<u>el</u> uh kwuhnt) *adj.*
expressing oneself or itself clearly and smoothly
Synonyms: articulate, expressive

INSUFFERABLY (in <u>suhf</u> ur-uh blee) *adv.*
in a way that is too much to bear
Synonyms: unbearably, unacceptably,
horribly, outrageously

CHAPTER 8

What a hero Tom had become, now! He did not go skipping and prancing, but he moved with a **dignified** walk as became a pirate who felt that the public eye was on him. At school the children made so much of him and of Joe and delivered such **eloquent** admiration from their eyes, that the two heroes were not long in becoming **insufferably** stuck-up.

Tom decided that he could be rid of Becky Thatcher now. Glory was enough. He

DISTINGUISHED (diss <u>ting</u> gwisht) *adj.*
standing out in a positive way
Synonyms: famous, renowned, notable

FLUSHED (fluhshd) *adj.*
turned red in color
Synonyms: blushed, reddened

IRRESOLUTELY (i reh zuh <u>loot</u> lee) *adv.*
without making a decision about what to do
Synonyms: uncertainly, undecidedly,
indecisively

would live for glory. Now that he was **distinguished**, maybe she would want to make up.

Presently Becky arrived. Tom pretended not to see her. He moved away and joined a group of boys and girls and began to talk. Soon he observed that she was tripping happily back and forth with **flushed** face and dancing eyes, pretending to be busy chasing schoolmates and screaming with laughter when she made a capture. But he noticed that she always made her captures in his area. He also noticed that she seemed to cast an eye in his direction at such times, too. Instead of winning him, however, all this only "set him up" the more and made want even more to avoid betraying that he knew what she was doing.

Presently Becky moved **irresolutely** about, sighing once or twice and glancing secretly toward Tom. Then she observed that Tom was now talking more to Amy Lawrence than to any one else. That was the girl he had once been "engaged" to. Becky felt a sharp pain and grew uneasy at once.

SHAM (sham) *adj.*
　　false or fake
　　　　Synonyms: fake, phony, mock

VIVACITY (vi <u>vass</u> i tee) *n.*
　　the state of having energy
　　　　Synonyms: spirit, exuberance, animation

She spoke to a girl almost at Tom's elbow, saying, with **sham vivacity**:

"Why, Mary Austin! you bad girl, why didn't you come to Sunday school?"

"I did come – didn't you see me?"

"Why, no! Did you? Where did you sit?"

"I was in Miss Peters' class, where I always go. I saw YOU."

"Did you? Why, it's funny I didn't see you. I wanted to tell you about the picnic."

"Oh, that's jolly. Who's going to give it?"

"My ma's going to let me have one."

"Oh, good. I hope she'll let ME come."

"Well, she will. The picnic's for me. She'll let anybody come that I want, and I want you."

"That's ever so nice. When is it going to be?"

"By and by. Maybe about vacation time."

"Oh, won't it be fun! You going to have all the girls and boys?"

"Yes, every one that's friends to me – or wants to be" – and she glanced ever so furtively at Tom.

"Oh, may I come?" said Grace Miller.

"Yes."

VINDICTIVE (vin <u>dik</u> tiv) *adj.*
   intending revenge
      Synonyms: malicious, vengeful, spiteful

FLIRTATION (flur <u>tay</u> shuhn) *n.*
   the act of being romantic with someone
   without serious intent
      Synonym: toying

LACERATE (<u>la</u> suh rayt) *v.* **-ing**, **-ed**
   to cause sharp emotional pain
      Synonyms: torment, torture, agonize

"And me?" said Sally Rogers.

"Yes."

"And me, too?" said Susy Harper. "And Joe?"

"Yes."

And so on, with clapping of joyful hands until all the group had begged for invitations but Tom and Amy. Then Tom turned coolly away, still talking, and took Amy with him. Becky's lips trembled and the tears came to her eyes. She hid these signs with a forced happiness and went on chattering, but the life had gone out of the picnic, now, and out of everything else. She got away as soon as she could and hid herself. Then she sat moody, with wounded pride, till the bell rang. She roused up, now, with a **vindictive** cast in her eye, and gave her hair a shake and said she knew what SHE'D do.

At recess Tom continued his **flirtation** with Amy with self-satisfaction. And he kept drifting about to find Becky and **lacerate** her with the performance. At last he spied her, but there was a sudden falling of his strength of mind. She was sitting comfortably on a little bench behind

ABSORBED (uhb <u>zorbd</u>) *adj.*
 deeply interested or lost in something
  Synonyms: immersed, captivated

RECONCILIATION (re kuhn si lee <u>ay</u> shuhn) *n.*
 the act of making up after a fight
  Synonyms: peace-making, settlement

VEXATION (vek <u>say</u> shuhn) *n.*
 the condition of being irritated
  Synonyms: displeasure, aggravation

the schoolhouse looking at a picture-book with Alfred Temple, the new boy with whom Tom had had his battle. Becky and Alfred looked so **absorbed**, with their heads so close together over the book, that they did not seem to be conscious of anything in the world besides. Jealousy ran red-hot through Tom's veins. He began to hate himself for throwing away the chance Becky had offered for **reconciliation**. He called himself a fool and all the other hard names he could think of. He wanted to cry with **vexation**.

"Any other boy!" Tom thought, grating his teeth. "Any boy in the whole town but that Saint Louis smarty! Oh, all right, I licked you the first day you ever saw this town, mister, and I'll lick you again! You just wait till I catch you! I'll just take and—"

He went through the motions of <u>thrashing</u> an imaginary boy, hitting the air, and kicking and punching. "Oh, you do, do you? You holler 'nuff, do you? Now, then, let that learn you!" And so the imaginary beating was finished to his satisfaction.

ENDURE (en <u>dur</u>) *v.* **-ing**, **-ed**
to put up with something unpleasant or painful
Synonyms: tolerate, bear

MISERABLE (<u>miz</u> ruh buhl) *adj.*
in a state of unhappiness
Synonym: heartbroken

Tom fled home at noon. His conscience could not **endure** any more of Amy's grateful happiness, and his jealousy could bear no more of the other distress.

Becky resumed her picture observing with Alfred, but as the minutes dragged along and no Tom came to suffer, her triumph began to cloud and she lost interest. Absent-mindedness followed, and then melancholy. Two or three times she pricked up her ear at a footstep, but it was a false hope. No Tom came. At last she grew **miserable** and wished she hadn't carried it so far. Then she burst into tears. Alfred dropped alongside and was going to try to comfort her, but she said:

"Go away and leave me alone, can't you! I hate you!"

So the boy halted, wondering what he could have done, for she had said she would look at pictures all through the afternoon. She walked on, crying. Then Alfred went sadly into the deserted schoolhouse. He was angry. He easily guessed his way to the truth. The girl had simply made a

CONVENIENCE (kuhn <u>vee</u> nyuhnss) *n.*
something that is suitable for a short time
Synonyms: advantage, luxury

SCORCH (skorch) *v.* **-ing**, **-ed**
to cause intense mental pain
Synonyms: burn, sear

RESOLVE (ri <u>zolv</u>) *v.* **-ing**, **-ed**
to reach a final decision
Synonyms: decide, conclude, determine

convenience of him to vent her spite upon Tom Sawyer. He was far from hating Tom the less when this thought came to him. He wished there was some way to get that boy into trouble without much risk to himself. Tom's spelling book fell under his eye. Here was his chance. He gratefully opened to the lesson for the afternoon and poured ink upon the page.

Becky, glancing in at a window behind him at the moment, saw the act and moved on, without revealing herself. She started homeward, now, intending to find Tom and tell him. Tom would be thankful and their troubles would be healed. Before she was half way home, however, she had changed her mind. The thought of Tom's treatment of her when she was talking about her picnic came **scorching** back and filled her with shame. She **resolved** to let him get whipped on the damaged spelling book's account, and to hate him forever, into the bargain.

DREARY (<u>drih</u> ree) *adj.*
gloomy, comfortless
Synonyms: glum

ESTABLISH (ess <u>tab</u> lish) *v.* **-ing**, **-ed**
to confirm something to be accurate
Synonyms: find, discover

CHAPTER 9

Tom arrived at home in a **dreary** mood, and the first thing his aunt said to him showed him that he had brought his sorrows to an unpromising market:

"Tom, I've a notion to skin you alive!"

"Auntie, what have I done?"

"Well, you've done enough. Here I go over to Sereny Harper, like an old softy, expecting I'm going to make her believe all that rubbish about that dream, when lo and behold you, she'd **established** from Joe that you was over here and

ASSUME (uh <u>soom</u>) *v.* **-ing**, **-ed**
to accept something to be true without
confirming it
Synonyms: suppose, imagine, believe

heard all the talk we had that night. Tom, I don't know what is to become of a boy that will act like that. It makes me feel so bad to think you could let me go to Sereny Harper and make such a fool of myself and never say a word."

He hung his head and could not think of anything to say for a moment. Then he said:

"Auntie, I wish I hadn't done it – but I didn't think."

"Oh, child, you never think. You never think of anything but your own selfishness. You could **assume** to come all the way over here from Jackson's Island in the night to laugh at our troubles, and you could think to fool me with a lie about a dream. But you couldn't ever think to pity us and save us from sorrow."

"I didn't come over here to laugh at you that night."

"What did you come for, then?"

"It was to tell you not to be uneasy about us, because we hadn't got drowned."

"Tom, Tom, I would be the thankfullest soul in this world if I could believe you ever had as

TENDERNESS (<u>ten</u> dur nuhss) *n.*
   a state of being fond of someone or something
      Synonyms: care, compassion

TREMOR (<u>trem</u> ur) *n.*
   a trembling or quivering movement
      Synonyms: vibration, shiver, shake

good a thought as that, but you know you never did, and I know it, Tom."

"Indeed and 'deed I did, auntie, I wish I may never stir if I didn't."

"Oh, Tom, don't lie – don't do it. It only makes things a hundred times worse."

"Why, you see, when you got to conversing about the funeral, I just got all full of the idea of our coming and hiding in the church, and I couldn't somehow bear to spoil it. So I just put the bark back in my pocket and kept <u>mum</u>."

"What bark?"

"The bark I had wrote on to tell you we'd gone pirating. I wish, now, you'd waked up when I kissed you – I do, honest."

The hard lines in his aunt's face relaxed and a sudden **tenderness** dawned in her eyes.

"DID you kiss me, Tom?"

"Why, yes, I did."

The words sounded like truth. The old lady could not hide a **tremor** in her voice when she said:

"Kiss me again, Tom! – and be off with you to school, now, and don't bother me any more."

REFRAIN (ri <u>frayn</u>) *v.* **-ing**, **-ed**
to stop from doing something
Synonyms: cease, desist

VENTURE (<u>ven</u> chur) *v.* **-ing**, **-ed**
to attempt something daring
Synonyms: risk, chance, dare

The moment he was gone, she ran to a closet and got out the ruin of a jacket which Tom had gone pirating in. Then she stopped with it in her hand and said to herself:

"No, I don't dare. Poor boy, I reckon he's lied about it – but it's a blessed, blessed lie, there's such a comfort come from it. I hope the Lord will forgive him because it was such good heart in him to tell it. But I don't want to find out it's a lie. I won't look."

She put the jacket away and stood by musing a minute. Twice she put out her hand to take the garment again, and twice she **refrained**. Once more she **ventured**, and this time she strengthened herself with the thought: "It's a good lie – it's a good lie – I won't let it grieve me." So she sought the jacket pocket. A moment later she was reading Tom's piece of bark through flowing tears and saying: "I could forgive the boy, now, if he'd committed a million sins!"

HESITATION (he zuh <u>tay</u> shun) *n.*
a pause before doing something
Synonyms: delay, reluctance, wavering

CHAPTER 10

There was something about Aunt Polly's manner when she kissed Tom that swept away his low spirits and made him happy again. He started to school and had the luck of coming upon Becky Thatcher at the head of Meadow Lane. His mood always determined his manner. Without a moment's **hesitation** he ran to her:

"I acted mighty mean today, Becky, and I'm so sorry. I won't ever, ever do that way again, as long as ever I live – please make up, won't you?"

ENCOUNTER (en <u>koun</u> turd) *v.* **-ing**, **-ed**
to meet someone
Synonyms: confront, face

BREACH (<u>breech</u>) *n.*
a break in a relationship
Synonyms: division, split

EXPOSE (ex <u>spoze</u>) *v.* **-ing**, **-ed**
to show something, to uncover the truth
Synonyms: reveal, disclose, make known

AMBITION (am <u>bih</u> shuhn) *n.*
a wish or desire, especially to be successful at
something
Synonyms: goal, objective, aspiration

POVERTY (<u>pov</u> ur tee) *n.*
the condition of being poor
Synonyms: deficiency, poorness

The girl stopped and looked him in the face:

"I'll thank you to keep yourself TO yourself, Mr. Thomas Sawyer. I'll never speak to you again."

She tossed her head and passed on. He <u>moped</u> into the schoolyard wishing she were a boy and imagining how he would beat her if she were. He presently **encountered** her and delivered a stinging remark as he passed. She hurled one in return, and the angry **breach** was complete. It seemed to Becky, in her hot anger, that she could hardly wait for school to "take in," she was so impatient to see Tom flogged for the injured spelling book. If she had had any notion of **exposing** Alfred Temple, Tom's actions and words had driven it away.

Poor girl, she did not know how fast she was nearing trouble herself. The master, Mr. Dobbins, had reached middle age with an unsatisfied **ambition**. The darling of his desires was to be a doctor, but **poverty** had made it that he should be nothing higher than a village schoolmaster. Every day he took a mysterious book out of his desk and absorbed himself in it at times when no

GLIMPSE (<u>glimpss</u>) *n.*
a very quick view of something
Synonyms: glance, peek

ENGRAVED (en <u>grayvd</u>) *adj.*
with a design cut into it
Synonyms: imprinted, carved

VEXATION (veks <u>ay</u> shun) *n.*
the state of being annoyed or upset
Synonyms: bother, strain, anxiety

classes were going. He kept that book under lock and key. There was not an <u>urchin</u> in school but was perishing to have a **glimpse** of it, but the chance never came. Every boy and girl had a theory about the nature of that book. No two theories were alike, and there was no way of getting at the facts in the case. Now, as Becky was passing by the desk, which stood near the door, she noticed that the key was in the lock! It was a great moment. She glanced around, found herself alone, and the next instant she had the book in her hands. The title-page – Professor Somebody's <u>ANATOMY</u> – carried no information to her mind; so she began to turn the leaves. She came at once upon a handsomely **engraved** and colored front piece – a human figure, stark naked.

At that moment a shadow fell on the page and Tom Sawyer stepped in at the door and caught a glimpse of the picture. Becky snatched at the book to close it and had the hard luck to tear the pictured page half down the middle. She thrust the volume into the desk, turned the key, and burst out crying with shame and **vexation**.

FLUSTERED (<u>fluhss</u> turrd) *adj.*

not processing something due to an unexpected event

Synonyms: confused, upset, bewildered

MALEVOLENT (muh <u>le</u> voh luhnt) *adj.*

having ill-will

Synonyms: malicious, spiteful, vengeful

"Tom Sawyer, you are just as mean as you can be to sneak up on a person and look at what they're looking at."

"How could I know you was looking at anything?"

"You ought to be ashamed of yourself, Tom Sawyer. You know you're going to tell on me, and oh, what shall I do, what shall I do! I'll be whipped, and I never was whipped in school."

Tom stood still, rather **flustered** by this attack. Presently he said to himself:

"What a curious kind of a fool a girl is! Never been whipped in school! Shucks! What's a whipping! Well, of course I ain't going to tell old Dobbins on this little fool because there's other ways of getting even on her that ain't so **malevolent**. But what of it? Old Dobbins will ask who it was tore his book. Nobody'll answer. Then he'll do just the way he always does – ask first one and then t'other, and when he comes to the right girl he'll know it, without any telling."

Tom thought about the thing a moment longer, and then added: "All right, though

CONSIDER (kuhn <u>sid</u> ur) *v.* **-ing**, **-ed**
to think about something carefully before
deciding what to do
Synonyms: contemplate, ponder

LETHARGY (<u>leh</u> thuhr jee) *n.*
a state of being without energy or movement
Synonyms: laziness, sluggishness, indolence

DISTRESS (diss <u>tress</u>) *n.*
a feeling of sadness or intense pain
Synonyms: sorrow, anguish, mortification

PROCEEDING (pruh <u>see</u> ding) *n.*
a course of action or events
Synonyms: business, case

she'd like to see me in just such a fix. Let her
sweat it out!"

In a few moments the master arrived and
school "took in." Every time he stole a glance at
the girls' side of the room Becky's face troubled
him. **Considering** all things, he did not want
to pity her, and yet it was all he could do to help
it. He could get up no joy that was really worthy
the name.

Presently the spelling book discovery was
made, and Tom's mind was full of his own mat-
ters for a while after that. Becky roused up from
her **lethargy** of **distress** and showed good interest in the **proceedings**. She did not expect that
Tom could get out of his trouble by denying that
he spilt the ink on the book himself, and she was
right. The denial only seemed to make the thing
worse for Tom. Becky supposed she would be glad
of that, and she tried to believe she was glad of it,
but she found she was not certain. When the worst
came to the worst, she had an impulse to get up
and tell on Alfred Temple, but she made an effort
and forced herself to keep still – because, said she

IMMINENCE (i̱ muh nuhnss) *n.*
the condition of something being about to occur
  Synonyms: nearness, eventuality, approach

PARALYZE (p̲a̲ ruh lize) *v.* **-ing**, **-ed**
to be unable to move or act
  Synonyms: immobilize, petrify

INSPIRATION (in spuh r̲a̲y̲ shuhn) *n.*
a sudden emotion or idea
  Synonyms: brainstorm, insight

RESOLUTION (rez uh l̲o̲o̲ shuhn) *n.*
the condition of being determined or having a fixed mind
  Synonyms: settlement, firmness

to herself, "he'll tell about me tearing the picture sure. I wouldn't say a word, not to save his life!"

Tom took his whipping and went back to his seat not at all broken hearted, for he thought it was possible that he had unknowingly upset the ink on the spelling book himself.

A whole hour drifted by, the master sat nodding in his throne, and the air was drowsy with the hum of study. Mr. Dobbins fingered his special book for a while, then took it out and settled himself in his chair to read! Tom shot a glance at Becky. He had seen a hunted and helpless rabbit look as she did, with a gun pointed at its head.

Instantly Tom forgot his argument with her. Quick – something must be done! done in a flash, too! But the very **imminence** of the emergency **paralyzed** him. Good! He had an **inspiration!** He would run and snatch the book, spring through the door and fly. But his **resolution** shook for one little instant, and the chance was lost – the master opened the volume. If Tom only had the wasted opportunity back again! Too late. There was no help for Becky now, he thought.

WRATH (<u>rath</u>) *n.*
intense anger
Synonyms: fury, rage

The next moment the master faced the school. Every eye sank under his gaze. There was that in it which smote even the innocent with fear. There was silence while one might count ten – the master was gathering his **wrath**. Then he spoke: "Who tore this book?"

There was not a sound. One could have heard a pin drop. The stillness continued. The master searched face after face for signs of guilt.

"Benjamin Rogers, did you tear this book?"

A denial. Another pause.

"Joseph Harper, did you?"

Another negative. The next person was Becky Thatcher. Tom was trembling from head to foot with excitement and a sense of the hopelessness of the situation.

"Rebecca Thatcher" (Tom glanced at her face – it was white with terror) – did you tear – no, look me in the face" (her hands rose in appeal) – "did you tear this book?"

A thought shot like lightning through Tom's brain. He sprang to his feet and shouted – "I done it!"

ADORATION (a duh <u>ray</u> shuhn) *n.*
fondness or love of someone
Synonyms: admiration, esteem, passion

MERCILESS (<u>mer</u> suh less) *adj.*
without mercy
Synonyms: pitiless, ruthless, harsh

INDIFFERENCE (in <u>dif</u> uhr uhnss) *n.*
the state of having no interest in certain affairs
Synonyms: apathy, irresponsiveness

DETENTION (di <u>ten</u> shun) *n.*
the state of being kept somewhere
Synonyms: confinement, restraint

VENGEANCE (<u>ven</u> juhnss) *n.*
an act of revenge
Synonyms: retaliation, repayment

TREACHERY (<u>trech</u> uh ree) *n.*
a disloyal act
Synonyms: deceit, disloyalty

Tom stood a moment to gather his senses. When he stepped forward to go to his punishment, the surprise and the **adoration** that shone upon him out of poor Becky's eyes seemed pay enough for a hundred whippings. Inspired by the greatness of his own act, he took without an outcry the most **merciless** beating that even Mr. Dobbins had ever given. He also received with **indifference** the added cruelty of a command to remain two hours after school was dismissed – for he knew who would wait for him outside till his **detention** was done, and not count the time as loss, either.

Tom went to bed that night planning **vengeance** against Alfred Temple. For with shame and regret Becky had told him all, not forgetting her own **treachery**. But even the longing for revenge had to give way, soon, to better thoughts, and he fell asleep at last with Becky's latest words remaining dreamily in his ear—

"Tom, how COULD you be so noble!"

SEVERE (suh <u>veer</u>) *adj.*
of a hard or violent nature
Synonyms: brutal, ruthless, relentless

CHAPTER 11

Vacation was approaching. The schoolmaster grew more **severe** than ever, for he wanted the school to make a good showing on "Examination Day." His beating rod was never idle now – at least among the smaller pupils.

As the great day approached, all the anger that was in him came to the surface. He seemed to take a vindictive pleasure in punishing the least mistakes. The consequence was that the smaller boys spent their days in terror and suffering and their nights plotting revenge. They threw away

RETRIBUTION (reh truh <u>byoo</u> shuhn) *n.*
something given as punishment
Synonyms: vengeance, payback

SCHEME (<u>skeem</u>) *n.*
a plan to do something
Synonyms: plot, strategy

INTERFERE (in tur <u>fihr</u>) *v.* **-ing**, **-ed**
to hinder something from happening
Synonyms: meddle, obstruct, impede

no opportunity to do the master a mischief. But he kept ahead all the time. The **retribution** that followed every success was so sweeping that the boys always left from the field badly injured. At last they plotted together and hit upon a plan that promised a great victory.

The boys made the sign-painter's son take an oath of secrecy. Then they told him the **scheme** and asked his help. He had his own reasons for being happy about the plan, for the schoolmaster stayed in the house of his father's family and had given the boy enough cause to hate him. The schoolmaster's wife would go on a visit to the country in a few days, and there would be nothing to **interfere** with the plan. The master always prepared himself for great occasions by getting pretty drunk. The sign-painter's boy said that when the schoolmaster got drunk on the evening of the Examination Day activities he would "manage the thing" while the teacher napped in his chair. Then he would have the man woken up at the right time and hurried away to school.

In the fullness of time the interesting occasion

MELLOW (<u>mel</u> oh) *adj.*
relaxed, often from drinking liquor
Synonym: placid

INTOLERABLE (in <u>tol</u> ur uh buhl) *adj.*
not able to be endured or put up with
Synonyms: unbearable, unendurable

GESTURE (<u>jess</u> chur) *n.*
a movement used to express emotion
Synonyms: motion, gesticulation

arrived. At eight in the evening the schoolhouse was beautifully lighted and decorated with flowers. The master sat in his great chair upon a raised platform, with his blackboard behind him. He was looking **mellow**. Three rows of benches on each side and six rows in front of him were filled by the wise men of the town and by the parents of the students. To his left, back of the rows of citizens, was a platform upon which were seated the students who were to take part in the exercises of the evening. There were rows of small boys, washed and dressed to an **intolerable** state of discomfort, rows of big boys, and snowbanks of girls and young ladies clearly conscious of their bare arms, their grandmothers' ancient jewels, their bits of pink and blue ribbon and the flowers in their hair. All the rest of the house was filled with uninvolved students.

The exercises began. A very little boy stood up and sheepishly recited, "You'd scarce expect one of my age to speak in public on the stage," etc. He carried himself with the painfully exact and jerky **gestures** which a machine might have

INDESTRUCTIBLE (in di <u>struhk</u> tuh buhl) *adj.*
unable to be ruined or destroyed
Synonyms: unbreakable, enduring,
immortal

GESTICULATION (jess tik yuh <u>lay</u> shuhn) *n.*
wild movement of the arms to express
something with excitement or anger
Synonyms: gesture, wave, motion

RECITE (ri <u>site</u>) *v.* **-ing, -ed**
to speak something aloud from memory
Synonyms: chant, parrot, perform

used – supposing the machine to be a bit out of order. But he got through safely, though very scared, and got a fine round of applause when he made his bow and retired.

A little shamefaced girl lisped, "Mary had a little lamb," etc., performed a pitiful curtsy, got her applause, and sat down flushed and happy.

Tom Sawyer stepped forward with confidence and soared into the **indestructible** "Give me liberty or give me death" speech, with fine fury and frantic **gesticulation** and then broke down in the middle of it. A nasty stage-fright froze him, his legs shook under him, and he was like to choke. True, he had the sympathy of the house, but he had the house's silence, too, which was even worse than its sympathy. The master frowned, and this completed the disaster. Tom struggled awhile and then retired, defeated. There was a weak attempt at applause, but it died early.

"The Boy Stood on the Burning Deck" followed, also "The Assyrian Came Down," and other readings. Then there were reading exercises, and a spelling bee. The Latin class **recited** with honor.

FEATURE (<u>fee</u> chur) *n.*
a special attraction
Synonyms: highlight, speciality

PUNCTUATION (puhngk choo <u>ay</u> shuhn) *n.*
the use of breaks and pauses in a composition
Synonyms: pause, articulation

RECOLLECTION (rek uh <u>lek</u> shuhn) *n.*
an event or thing that is remembered
Synonyms: memory, reminiscence

The main **feature** of the evening was pieces by the young ladies. Each in her turn stepped forward to the edge of the platform, cleared her throat, held up her writing (tied with pretty ribbon), and read, with attention to "expression" and **punctuation**. The first piece that was read was one called:

"A Missouri Maiden's Farewell To Alabama"

"Alabama, good-bye! I love thee well! But yet for a while do I leave thee now! Sad, yes, sad thoughts of thee my heart does swell, and burning **recollections** crowd my mind! For I have walked through thy flowery woods. I have wandered and read near the stream. I have listened to the floods.

"Yet shame I not to bear an o'er-full heart, nor blush to turn behind my tearful eyes. 'Tis from no stranger land I now must part, 'tis to no strangers left I yield these sighs. Welcome and home were mine within this State, whose valley I leave – whose towers fade fast from me, and cold must be mine eyes, and heart, and mind, when, dear Alabama! they turn cold on thee!"

The piece was very good. Next appeared a dark, black-eyed, black-haired young lady, who

TEMPESTUOUS (tem <u>pes</u> choo uhss) *adj.*
in the manner of a storm or tempest
Synonyms: stormy, blustery, turbulent

EXERT (eg <u>zurt</u>) *v.* **-ing**, **-ed**
to put forth
Synonyms: push, struggle

GENIAL (<u>jeen</u> yuhl) *adj.*
courteous and friendly
Synonyms: amiable, welcoming, nice

146

paused a moment, put on a sad face, and began to read in a sad tone:

"A Vision."

"Dark and **tempestuous** was night. Around the throne on high not a single star shook. But the deep heavy thunder smashed upon the ear, whilst the lightning struck in angry mood through the cloudy space of heaven, seeming to hate the power **exerted** over its terror by human control of lightening! Even the lively winds came forth from their magic homes, and blew about as if to add by their aid to the wildness of the scene.

"At such a time, so dark for human sympathy my very spirit sighed. But instead thereof, "'My dearest friend, my guide – my joy in grief, my second bliss in joy came to my side. She moved like one of those bright beings pictured in the sunny walks of heaven by the romantic and young, a queen of beauty. So soft was her step it failed to make even a sound. And but for the magical thrill given by her **genial** touch, as other unseen beauties, she would have glided away unseen and not chased. A strange sadness rested

CONTENDING (kuhn <u>tend</u> ing) *adj.*
 to compete with something
  Synonyms: challenging, opposing

DISTORT (diss <u>tort</u>) *v.* **-ing**, **-ed**
 to twist something out of shape
  Synonyms: deform, fudge, mangle

SUSPENDED (suh <u>spend</u> ed) *adj.*
 kept from falling by being attached to
 something else
  Synonyms: hung, hovered, dangled

upon her, like icy tears upon the robe of December, as she pointed to the **contending** elements without, and bade me contemplate the two beings presented."

This nightmare occupied some ten pages and wound up with a sermon that took the first prize.

Now the master, mellow almost to the point of geniality, put his chair aside, turned his back to the audience, and began to draw a map of America on the blackboard. He would quiz the <u>geography</u> class upon it. But he made a sad business of it with his unsteady hand. He knew what the matter was, and he set himself to right it. He took out lines and remade them, but he only **distorted** them more than ever. He threw all his attention upon his work, now, as if determined not to be put down by the fun. He felt that all eyes were upon him. He imagined he was succeeding, and yet the giggling continued. It even increased. And well it might. There was a loft above, with a hole over his head, and down through this hole came a cat, **suspended** around the back legs by a string. She had a rag tied about her head and jaws to keep her from

POSSESSION (puh <u>zesh</u> uhn) *n.*
an item owned by someone
Synonyms: ownership, custody

AVENGED (uh <u>venjd</u>) *adj.*
satisfied from taking revenge on someone
Synonyms: retaliated, settled

mewing. As she slowly dropped down she curved upward and clawed at the string. She swung downward and clawed at the air. The giggling rose higher and higher – the cat was within six inches of the teacher's head – down, down, a little lower. Then she grabbed his wig with her claws, clung to it, and was snatched up into the hole in an instant with her trophy still in her **possession**! And how the light did shine from the master's bald head – for the sign-painter's boy had painted it a gleaming gold!

That broke up the meeting. The boys were **avenged**. Vacation had come.

SECONDARY (<u>sek</u> uhn der ee) *adj.*
less important, not of the first rank
Synonyms: minor, lesser, inferior

PECULIARLY (pi <u>kyoo</u> lyur lee) *adv.*
done in an unusual way
Synonyms: abnormally, weirdly

CHAPTER 12

The first thing Tom heard on Friday morning several weeks later was a glad piece of news – Judge Thatcher's family had come back to town the night before after a brief trip away. Everything else sank into **secondary** importance for a moment, and Becky took the chief place in the boy's interest. He saw her, and they had an exhausting good time playing with their schoolmates. The day was completed and crowned in a **peculiarly** pleasing way. Becky had <u>teased</u> her mother to choose the next day for the

CONSENT (kuhn <u>sent</u>) *v.* **-ing**, **-ed**
    to agree to something
        Synonyms: approve, give in, assent

ENABLE (en <u>ay</u> buhl) *v.* **-ing**, **-ed**
    to make it possible for something to happen
        Synonyms: permit, allow

PRESENCE (<u>prez</u> uhnss) *n.*
    the state of being somewhere at a certain time
        Synonyms: attendance, proximity

CHARTER (<u>char</u> tur) *v.* **-ing**, **-ed**
    to pay money for rental of something or some
    place for a special occasion
        Synonyms: rent, hire

long-promised picnic, and Mrs. Thatcher had finally **consented**. The child's delight in the picnic was endless, and Tom's was not any smaller.

The invitations were sent out before sunset, and straightway the young folks of the village were thrown into a fever of preparation. Tom and Huck had planned to go hunting for treasure, and they planned for Huck to "meow" like a cat if there were any good leads. His excitement **enabled** him to keep awake until a pretty late hour, and he had good hopes of hearing Huck's "meow" and of having his treasure to surprise Becky and the picnickers with the next day. He was disappointed. No signal came that night. However the thought of the coming picnic kept him happy.

Morning came, eventually, and by ten or eleven o'clock an excited company was gathered at Judge Thatcher's. Everything was ready for a start. It was not the custom for old people to ruin the picnics with their **presence**. The old steam ferryboat was **chartered** for the occasion, and presently the group filed up the main street with baskets of food. Sid was sick and had to miss the fun, and

ENTERTAIN (en tur <u>tayn</u>) *v.* **-ing**, **-ed**
   to keep someone company
     Synonyms: interest, amuse, keep busy

SPLENDID (<u>splen</u> did) *adj.*
   extremely impressive
     Synonyms: superb, marvelous

Cousin Mary remained at home to **entertain** him. The last thing Mrs. Thatcher said to Becky, was:

"You'll not get back till late. Perhaps you'd better stay all night with some of the girls that live near the ferry landing, child."

"Then I'll stay with Susy Harper, mamma."

"Very well. And mind and behave yourself and don't be any trouble."

Presently, as they tripped along, Tom said to Becky:

"Say – I'll tell you what we'll do. 'Stead of going to Joe Harper's we'll climb right up the hill and stop at the Widow Douglas'. She'll have ice cream! She has it most every day – dead loads of it. And she'll be awful glad to have us."

"Oh, that will be fun!"

The Widow Douglas' **splendid** hospitality was tempting bait. So it was decided to say nothing to anybody about the night's program.

Three miles below town the ferryboat stopped at the mouth of a woody hollow and tied up. The crowd swarmed ashore and soon the forest distances and mountain heights echoed far and

REFRESHING (ri <u>fresh</u> ing) *adj.*
giving one a sense of youth and freshness
Synonyms: uplifting, energizing

PROCURE (pro <u>kyoor</u>) *v.* **-ing**, **-ed**
to take possession of something with effort
Synonyms: acquire, gain, find

near with shouting and laughter. All the different ways of getting hot and tired were gone through, and by and by the wanderers made their way back to camp with hearty appetites. After the feast there was a **refreshing** season of rest and chat in the shade of spreading oaks. By and by somebody shouted:

"Who's ready for the cave?"

Everybody was. The town's tradition of traveling to the cave excited both young boys and grown men alike. Volunteers **procured** bundles of candles, and straightaway there was a general run up the hill. The mouth of the cave was up the hillside – an opening shaped like a letter A. Its large door stood unbarred. Within was a small chamber, chilly as an <u>ice house</u>, and walled by Nature with solid stone that was damp with a cold sweat. It was romantic and mysterious to stand here in the deep darkness and look out upon the green valley shining in the sun. But the greatness of the situation quickly wore off, and the romping began again. The moment a candle was lighted there was a general rush upon the owner of it. A

GALLANT (<u>gal</u> uhnt) *adj.*
without fear
Synonyms: valiant, heroic

DESCENT (di <u>sent</u>) *n.*
a downward slope
Synonyms: drop, plunge

CREVICE (<u>krev</u> iss) *n.*
a crack or split in a rock or surface
Synonyms: gap, fissure, fracture

LABYRINTH (<u>lab</u> uhr inth) *n.*
a place that is full of complicated passageways
Synonyms: maze, puzzle

CHASM (<u>kaz</u> uhm) *n.*
a deep crack in the earth's surface
Synonyms: gorge, break, fissure

struggle and a **gallant** defense followed, but the candle was soon knocked down or blown out, and then there was a glad laughter and a new chase. But all things have an end. By and by the procession went filing down the steep **descent** of the main avenue, the flickering rank of lights revealing the lofty walls of rock almost to where they joined sixty feet overhead. This main avenue was not more than eight or ten feet wide. Every few steps other lofty and still narrower **crevices** branched from it on either hand – for McDougal's Cave was **labyrinth** of crooked tunnels that ran into each other and out again and led nowhere.

It was said that one might wander for days and nights through its tangle of **chasms** and never find the end of the cave. It was also said that one might go down and down and still further down into the earth, and it was just the same – labyrinth under labyrinth and no end to any of them. No man "knew" the cave. That was an impossible thing. Most of the young men knew a portion of it, and it was not customary to venture much beyond

CORRIDOR (<u>kor</u> uh dur) *n.*
a long passageway
Synonyms: walkway, hall, passage

ELUDE (i <u>lude</u>) *v.* **-ing, -ed**
to avoid being around someone or something
Synonyms: evade, dodge, ignore

this known part. Tom Sawyer knew as much of the cave as any one.

The procession moved along the main avenue some three-quarters of a mile, and then groups and couples began to slip aside into avenues. They flew along the haunting **corridors**, taking each other by surprise at points where the corridors joined again. Parties were able to **elude** each other for the space of half an hour without going beyond the "known" ground.

By and by, one group after another came straggling back to the mouth of the cave. The ringing bell had been calling for half an hour. When the ferryboat with her wild freight pushed into the stream, nobody cared for the wasted time but the captain of the craft.

There was no Sunday school during day school vacation, but everybody was early at church. The stirring event was well attended. When the sermon was finished, Judge Thatcher's wife dropped alongside of Mrs. Harper as she moved down the aisle with the crowd and said:

FEEBLY (<u>fee</u> blee) *adv.*
   done in a weak way
      Synonyms: pathetically, half-heartedly

ANXIETY (ang <u>zye</u> uh tee) *n.*
   a feeling of concern or worry
      Synonyms: nervousness, fear, dread

"Is my Becky going to sleep all day? I just expected she would be tired to death."

"Your Becky?"

"Yes," with a startled look, "didn't she stay with you last night?"

"Why, no."

Mrs. Thatcher turned pale and sank into a pew just as Aunt Polly, talking quickly with a friend, passed by. Aunt Polly said:

"Good-morning, Mrs. Thatcher. Good-morning, Mrs. Harper. I've got a boy that's turned up missing. I reckon my Tom stayed at your house last night – one of you. And now he's afraid to come to church. I've got to settle with him."

Mrs. Thatcher shook her head **feebly** and turned paler than ever.

"He didn't stay with us," said Mrs. Harper, beginning to look uneasy. A marked **anxiety** came into Aunt Polly's face.

"Joe Harper, have you seen my Tom this morning?"

"No'm."

"When did you see him last?"

COUNTENANCE (<u>koun</u> tuh nuhnss) *n.*
an expression on the face
Synonym: appearance

INQUIRE (in <u>kwire</u>) *v.* **-ing**, **-ed**
to request information
Synonyms: probe, question, investigate

TEDIOUS (<u>tee</u> dee uhss) *adj.*
moving slowly
Synonyms: monotonous, tiresome,
worrisome

Joe tried to remember, but he was not sure he could say. The people had stopped moving out of church. Whispers passed along, and uneasiness took possession of every **countenance**. Children were questioned, as were young teachers. They all said they had not noticed whether Tom and Becky were on board the ferryboat on the homeward trip. It was dark, and no one **inquired** if any one was missing. One young man finally blurted out his fear that they were still in the cave! Aunt Polly fell to crying.

The alarm swept from lip to lip, from group to group, from street to street. Within five minutes the bells were wildly chiming, and the whole town was up! Horses were saddled, the ferryboat ordered out, and before the horror was half an hour old, two hundred men were pouring down the road and river toward the cave.

All the long afternoon the village seemed empty and dead. Many women visited Aunt Polly and Mrs. Thatcher and tried to comfort them. They cried with them, too, and that was still better than words. All the **tedious** night the town waited

ENCOURAGEMENT (en <u>kur</u> ij muhnt) *n.*
the act of supporting someone
Synonym: inspiration

CONVEY (kuhn <u>vay</u>) *v.* **-ing**, **-ed**
to give someone a message
Synonyms: express, communicate, impart

MAZE (mayz) *n.*
a tangle of twisted lines or paths
Synonyms: labyrinth, knot, network

REVERBERATION (ri vur buh <u>ray</u> shun) *n.*
a vibration
Synonyms: impact, echo, sound

TRAVERSE (tra <u>verse</u>) *v.* **-ing**, **-ed**
to move through something
Synonyms: navigate, travel, cross

for news. But when the morning dawned at last, all the word that came was, "Send more candles – and send food." Mrs. Thatcher was almost crazed, and Aunt Polly was, also. Judge Thatcher sent messages of hope and **encouragement** from the cave, but they **conveyed** no real cheer.

Early noon, parties of men began to come into the village, but the strongest of the citizens continued searching. All the news that could be gained was that places in the cavern were being explored that had never been visited before. Every corner and crevice was going to be thoroughly searched. Wherever one wandered through the **maze** of passages, lights were to be seen here and there in the distance, and shoutings and pistol shots sent their **reverberations** to the ear down the quiet caverns. In one place, far from the section usually **traversed** by tourists, the names "BECKY & TOM" had been found traced upon the rocky wall with candle-smoke. Near at hand was a grease-stained bit of ribbon. Mrs. Thatcher recognized the ribbon and cried over it. She said it was the last item she should ever have of her child and that

PRECIOUS (<u>presh</u> uhss) *adj.*
   important to someone
      Synonyms: prized, treasured, irreplacable

STUPOR (<u>stoo</u> puhr) *n.*
   a state of mental paralysis in which nothing is
   done or thought
      Synonyms: trance, daze, lethargy

no other memorial of her could ever be so **precious**, because this one parted latest from the living body before the awful death came. Now and then, in the cave, a far-away speck of light would shine. Then a shout would burst forth, and a <u>score</u> of men go trooping down the echoing aisle. But then a sickening disappointment always followed. The children were not there. It was only a searcher's light.

Three dreadful days and nights dragged their tedious hours along, and the village sank into a hopeless **stupor**. No one had heart for anything. Couldn't somebody could find Tom Sawyer and Becky? Ah, there aren't many left, now, that had hope enough, or strength enough, either, to go on searching.

MURKY (<u>mur</u> kee) *adj.*
full of darkness or mystery
Synonyms: gloomy, foggy, dim

FROLICKING (<u>frol</u> ik ing) *n.*
a happy play
Synonyms: cavorting, skipping

CHAPTER 13

Now to return to Tom and Becky's part in the picnic. They tripped along the **murky** aisles with the rest of the company, visiting the familiar wonders of the cave – wonders given rather over-descriptive names, such as "The Drawing-Room," "The Cathedral," "Aladdin's Palace," and so on. Presently the hide-and-seek **frolicking** began, and Tom and Becky engaged in it with happiness until the exertion began to grow a bit tiring. They smoked their names under

ILLUMINATE (i <u>loo</u> muh nate) *v.* **-ing**, **-ed**
to light something up
Synonyms: light, clarify

GRATIFICATION (grat i fi <u>kay</u> shuhn) *n.*
the fulfilling of someone's needs or happiness
Synonyms: delight, enjoyment, pleasure

NOVELTY (<u>nov</u> uhl tee) *n.*
something new, interesting, and unusual
Synonym: innovation

NUMEROUS (<u>noo</u> mur uhss) *adj.*
consisting of a large number
Synonyms: many, abundant, plentiful

an overhanging ledge and moved on. Presently they came to a place where a little stream of water trickled over another ledge and had, in the slow-dragging ages, formed a laced and ruffled waterfall in gleaming stone.

Tom squeezed his small body behind it in order to **illuminate** it for Becky's **gratification**. He found that it curtained a sort of steep natural stairway which was enclosed between narrow walls, and at once the ambition to be a discoverer seized him. Becky responded to his call, and they made a smoke mark for future guidance. Then they started upon their quest. They wound this way and that, going far down into the secret places in the cave. They made another mark and branched off in search of **novelties** to tell the upper world about.

In one place they found a spacious cavern from whose ceiling hung many shining rock formations the length of a man's leg. They walked all around it, wondering and admiring, and presently left by one of the **numerous** passages that led from the cavern. This soon brought them to

FUGITIVE (<u>fyoo</u> juh tiv) *n.*
a person who is running away to escape
something
Synonyms: renegade, deserter

PERILOUS (<u>per</u> uhl uss) *adj.*
causing danger or peril
Synonyms: hazardous, unsafe, dangerous

SUBTERRANEAN (sub torr <u>ay</u> nee an) *adj.*
below the surface of the earth
Synonym: underground

APPREHENSIVE (ap ri <u>hen</u> siv) *adj.*
with slight fear or worry
Synonyms: uneasy, nervous, anxious

a spring whose basin was covered in glittering
<u>crystals</u>. It was in the middle of a cavern whose
walls were supported by many pillars, which had
been formed by the joining together of great rock
formations. All this was the result of the endless
water-drip of centuries. Under the roof vast knots
of bats had packed themselves together, thousands
in a bunch. The lights disturbed the creatures, and
they came flocking down by hundreds, squeak-
ing and darting at the candles. The bats chased
the children a good distance. But the **fugitives**
plunged into every new passage that offered, and
at last they were rid of the **perilous** things. Tom
soon found a **subterranean** lake, which stretched
its dim length away until its shape was lost in the
shadows. Becky said:

"Why, I didn't notice, but it seems ever so
long since I heard any of the others."

"Come to think, Becky, we are away down
below them – and I don't know how far away north,
or south, or east, or whichever it is. We couldn't
hear them here."

Becky grew **apprehensive**.

APPALLING (a <u>pawl</u> ing) *adj.*
causing horror or shock
Synonyms: upsetting, frightening

"I wonder how long we've been down here, Tom. We better start back."

"Yes, I reckon we better. P'raps we better."

"Can you find the way, Tom? It's all a mixed-up crookedness to me."

"I reckon I could find it – but then the bats . . . "His voice trailed off a moment. "If they put our candles out it will be an awful fix. Let's try some other way so as not to go through there."

"Well. But I hope we won't get lost. It would be so awful!" and the girl shuddered at the thought of the **appalling** possibilities.

They started through a corridor and traversed it in silence a long way. They glanced at each new opening to see if there was anything familiar about the look of it. But they were all strange. Every time Tom made an examination, Becky would watch his face for an encouraging sign, and he would say cheerily:

"Oh, it's all right. This ain't the one, but we'll come to it right away!"

But he felt less and less hopeful with each failure, and presently he began to turn off into

DIVERGING (duh <u>vuhrj</u> ing) *adj.*
branching out from a path
Synonyms: swerving, departing, wandering

ANGUISH (<u>ang</u> gwish) *n.*
a feeling of distress or misery
Synonyms: agony, suffering, torment

PROFOUND (pruh <u>found</u>) *adj.*
very deep
Synonyms: bottomless, intense

CONSPICUOUS (kuhn <u>spik</u> yoo uhss) *adj.*
standing out and easily seen
Synonyms: obvious, noticeable, prominent

diverging avenues at sheer random in desperate hope of finding the one that was wanted. He still said it was "all right," but there was such a heavy dread at his heart that the words had lost their ring and sounded just as if he had said, "All is lost!"

Becky clung to his side in an **anguish** of fear. She tried hard to keep back the tears, but they would come. At last she said:

"Oh, Tom, never mind the bats, let's go back that way! We seem to get worse and worse off all the time."

"Listen!" said he.

Profound silence, silence so deep that even their breathings were **conspicuous** in the hush. Tom shouted. The call went echoing down the empty aisles and died out in the distance in a faint sound. It seemed like a ripple of mocking laughter.

"Oh, don't do it again, Tom, it is too horrid," said Becky.

"It is horrid, but I better, Becky. They might hear us, you know," and he shouted again.

The "might" confessed such weak hope that

INDECISION (in di <u>sizh</u> uhn) *n.*
a lack of being able to make up one's mind
Synonyms: doubt, hesitation

FRENZY (<u>fren</u> zee) *n.*
a fit of emotion
Synonyms: whirl, fury, tumult

it was an even chillier horror than the ghostly laughter. The children stood still and listened, but there was no result. Tom turned to backtrack at once and hurried his steps. It was but a little while before a certain **indecision** in his manner revealed another fearful fact to Becky – he could not find his way back!

"Oh, Tom, you didn't make any marks!"

"Becky, I was such a fool! Such a fool! I never thought we might want to come back! No – I can't find the way. It's all mixed up."

"Tom, Tom, we're lost! we're lost! We never can get out of this awful place! Oh, why DID we ever leave the others!"

She sank to the ground and burst into such a **frenzy** of crying that Tom was convinced that she might die or lose her reason. He sat down by her and put his arms around her. Tom begged her to pluck up hope again, and she said she could not. He fell to blaming himself for getting her into this miserable situation. This had a better effect. She said she would try to hope again and that she would get up and follow wherever he might lead

REVIVING (ri <u>vive</u> ing) *n.*
   the state of coming back to life
      Synonyms: revitalizing, energizing

ECONOMY (i <u>kon</u> uh mee) *n.*
   the careful use of things to cut down on waste
      Synonyms: cutback, saving

FATIGUE (fuh <u>teeg</u>) *n.*
   a state of great tiredness
      Synonyms: exhaustion, weariness

if only he would not talk like that any more. For he was no more to blame than she, she said.

So they moved on again – aimlessly, simply at random. All they could do was to move, keep moving. For a little while hope made a show of **reviving** – not with any reason to back it, but only because it is its nature to revive when the spring has not been taken out of it by age and familiarity with failure.

By and by Tom took Becky's candle and blew it out. This **economy** meant so much! Words were not needed. Becky understood, and her hope died again. She knew that Tom had a whole candle and three or four pieces in his pockets – yet he must save them.

Fatigue bore so heavily upon Becky that she drowsed off to sleep. Tom was grateful. He sat looking into her drawn face and saw it grow smooth and natural under the influence of pleasant dreams. By and by a smile dawned and rested there. The peaceful face brought peace and healing into his own spirit, and his thoughts wandered away to <u>bygone</u> times and dreamy

MUSING (<u>myoo</u> zing) *n.*
a state of deep thought
Synonyms: deliberation, rumination

GORGEOUS (<u>gor</u> juhss) *adj.*
very attractive or beautiful
Synonyms: dazzling, lovely

HALLUCINATION (huh loo suh <u>nay</u> shuhn) *n.*
a vision in one's mind that doesn't really exist
Synonyms: illusion, mirage, delusion

ESTIMATE (<u>ess</u> ti mate) *v.* **-ing, -ed**
to form an opinion about something
Synonyms: guess, calculate

memories. While he was deep in his **musings**, Becky woke up with a breezy little laugh – but it was stricken dead upon her lips, and a groan followed it.

"Oh, how COULD I sleep! I wish I never, never had waked! No! No, I don't, Tom! Don't look so! I won't say it again."

"I'm glad you've slept, Becky. You'll feel rested, now, and we'll find the way out."

"We can try, Tom. But I've seen such a **gorgeous** country in my **hallucination**. I reckon we are going there."

"Maybe not, maybe not. Cheer up, Becky, and let's go on trying."

They rose up and wandered along, hand in hand and hopeless. They tried to **estimate** how long they had been in the cave, but all they knew was that it seemed days and weeks. Yet it was plain that this could not be, for their candles were not gone yet.

A long time after this – they could not tell how long – Tom said they must go softly and listen for dripping water. They must find a spring. They

BRUTALLY (<u>broo</u> tuh lee) *adj.*
   violently and cruelly
      Synonyms: viciously, harshly

VORACIOUS (vor <u>ay</u> shuss) *adj.*
   having great hunger
      Synonyms: ravenous, gluttonous, greedy

MOIETY (<u>moy</u> uh tee) *n.*
   a portion or small part
      Synonyms: segment, fraction, share

found one presently, and Tom said it was time to rest again. Both were **brutally** tired, yet Becky said she thought she could go a little farther. She was surprised to hear Tom say no. She could not understand it. They sat down, and Tom fastened his candle to the wall in front of them with some clay. Thought was soon busy. Nothing was said for some time. Then Becky broke the silence:

"Tom, I am so hungry!"

Tom took something out of his pocket.

"Do you remember this?" said he.

Becky almost smiled.

"It's the piece of cake we shared at the picnic, Tom – the one we pretended was our wedding cake."

"I wish it was big as a barrel. It's all we've got."

"You saved it from the picnic for us to dream on, Tom, the way grown-up people do with wedding cake – but it'll be our—"

She dropped the sentence where it was. Tom divided the cake and Becky ate with **voracious** appetite while Tom nibbled at his **moiety**. There

PLETHORA (<u>pleth</u> ur uh) *n.*
an amount that is more than enough
Synonyms: excess, surplus

was a **plethora** of cold water to finish the feast with. Soon Becky suggested that they move on again. Tom was silent a moment. Then he said:

"Becky, can you bear it if I tell you something?"

Becky's face paled, but she thought she could.

"Well, then, Becky, we must stay here where there's water to drink. That little piece is our last candle!"

Becky gave loose to tears and screams. Tom did what he could to comfort her but with little effect. At length Becky said:

"Tom!"

"Well, Becky?"

"They'll miss us and hunt for us!"

"Yes, they will! Certainly they will!"

"Maybe they're hunting for us now, Tom."

"Why, I reckon maybe they are. I hope they are."

"When would they miss us, Tom?"

"When they get back to the boat, I reckon."

"Tom, it might be dark then. Would they notice that we hadn't come?"

PITILESSLY (<u>pit</u> uh less lee) *adv.*
  done without mercy
    Synonyms: ruthlessly, heartlessly

FEEBLE (<u>fee</u> buhl) *adj.*
  very weak
    Synonyms: fragile, frail, powerless

"I don't know. But anyway, your mother would miss you as soon as they got home."

A frightened look in Becky's face brought Tom to his senses, and he saw that he had made a mistake. Becky was not to have gone home that night! The children became silent and thoughtful. In a moment a new burst of grief from Becky showed Tom that the thing in his mind had struck hers also – that the Sabbath morning might be half spent before Mrs. Thatcher discovered that Becky was not at Mrs. Harper's.

The children fastened their eyes upon their bit of candle and watched it melt slowly and **pitilessly** away. They saw the half inch of <u>wick</u> stand alone at last and saw the **feeble** flame rise and fall, climb the thin column of smoke, linger at its top a moment, and then – the horror of utter darkness reigned!

CONSCIOUSNESS (<u>kon</u> shuhss ness) *n.*
the state of being awake or aware
Synonyms: awareness, realization

OPPRESSIVE (uh <u>press</u> iv) *adj.*
difficult to bear or endure
Synonyms: overwhelming, brutal, dismal

CHAPTER 14

How long afterward it was that Becky came to a slow **consciousness** that she was crying in Tom's arms, neither could tell. All that they knew was that, after what seemed a mighty stretch of time, both awoke out of a dead stupor of sleep and resumed their miseries once more. Tom said it might be Sunday, now – maybe Monday. He tried to get Becky to talk, but her sorrows were too **oppressive**. All her hopes were gone. Tom said that they must have been missed long ago and that no doubt the search was going on.

GROPE (grohp) *v.* **-ing**, **-ed**
to feel around to find something hard to see
Synonyms: probe, examine

NADIR (<u>nay</u> der) *n.*
the lowest point
Synonyms: depth, pit, bottom

EVIDENTLY (<u>ev</u> uh duhnt lee) *adv.*
in a way that is clearly seen or understood
Synonyms: clearly, plainly, obviously

By-and-by Tom said:

"SH! Did you hear that?"

Both held their breath and listened. There was a sound like the faintest, far-off shout. Instantly Tom answered it, and, leading Becky by the hand, he started **groping** down the corridor in its direction. Presently he listened again. Again the sound was heard, and it was apparently a little nearer.

"It's them!" said Tom, "they're coming! Come along, Becky – we're all right now!"

The joy of the prisoners was almost overwhelming. Their speed was slow, however, because cracks in the cave floor were somewhat common and had to be guarded against. They shortly came to one and had to stop. It might be three feet deep, or it might be a hundred. There was no passing it at any rate. Tom got down on his chest and reached as far down as he could. No **nadir**. They must stay there and wait until the searchers came. They listened. **Evidently** the distant shoutings were growing more distant! A moment or two more and they had gone altogether. The heart-sinking

NAVIGABLE (<u>nav</u> uh gub bul) *adj.*
able to be traversed or moved through
Synonyms: negotiable, passable

misery of it! Tom yelled until he was <u>hoarse</u>, but it was of no use. He talked hopefully to Becky. But an age of anxious waiting passed, and no sounds came again.

Now an idea struck him. There were some side passages near at hand. He took a kite string from his pocket, tied it to a rock. He and Becky started, Tom in the lead, unwinding the string as he groped along. At the end of twenty steps the corridor ended in a "jumping-off place." Tom got down on his knees and felt below and then as far around the corner as he could reach with his hands. The passage was not **navigable**. But Tom spotted a curious sight – a note on the wall that read, "Treasure lies in this cave for those bold enough to seek it."

Tom noted this discovery but moved on, knowing escape from the cave was more important than treasure-hunts. He would surely return, however.

He proposed to explore another passage. He felt willing to risk ghosts and all other terrors. But Becky was very weak. She said she would

IMPLORE (im <u>plore</u>) *v.* **-ing**, **-ed**
to beg or ask urgently
Synonyms: plead, beseech

DISTRESSED (diss <u>tressd</u>) *adj.*
feeling great sadness or pain
Synonyms: upset, anguished

wait, now, where she was, and die – it would not be long. She told Tom to go with the kite string and explore if he chose. But she **implored** him to come back every little while and speak to her. And she made him promise that when the awful time came, he would stay by her and hold her hand until all was over.

Tom kissed her, with a choking sensation in his throat, and he made a show of being confident of finding the searchers or an escape from the cave. Then he took the kite string in his hand and went groping down one of the passages on his hands and knees, **distressed** with hunger and sick with thoughts of coming doom.

WANE (wayn) *v.* **-ing**, **-ed**
to become less or smaller
Synonyms: shrink, decrease, dwindle

PETITIONER (puh <u>tish</u> uhn uhr) *n.*
one who makes a formal request or plea
Synonyms: inquirer, suitor, hopeful

AVOCATION (a voh <u>kay</u> shun) *n.*
a hobby or pastime
Synonyms: interest, diversion, activity

CHAPTER 15

Tuesday afternoon came and **waned** to the twilight. The village of St. Petersburg still mourned. The lost children had not been found. Public prayers had been offered up for them, as had many and many a private prayer that had the **petitioner's** whole heart in it. But still no goodnews came from the cave. The majority of the searchers had given up the quest and gone back to their daily **avocations**, saying that it was plain the children could never be found. Mrs. Thatcher was very ill, and a great part of the time she was

DELIRIOUS (di <u>lihr</u> ee uhss) *adj.*

unable to reason

Synonyms: fevered, rambling, hallucinating

FORLORN (for <u>lorn</u>) *adj.*

lonely or unhappy

Synonyms: despondent, dejected, depressed

FRANTIC (<u>fran</u> tik) *adj.*

wildly excited, usually by fear or worry

Synonyms: excited, agitated

delirious. Aunt Polly had drooped into a settled melancholy, and her gray hair had grown almost white. The village went to its rest on Tuesday night, sad and **forlorn**.

In the middle of the night, however, a wild ring burst from the village bells. In a moment the streets were swarming with **frantic**, half-clad people who shouted, "Turn out! turn out! They're found! They're found!"

Tin pans and horns were added to the noise, and the population massed itself and moved toward the river. Then they met Tom and Becky coming in an open carriage drawn by shouting citizens. Townspeople crowded around it, joined its homeward march, and swept up the main street roaring hurray after hurray!

The village was illuminated. Nobody went to bed again, for it was the greatest night the little town had ever seen. During the first half-hour villagers filed through Judge Thatcher's house, seized the saved ones and kissed them, squeezed Mrs. Thatcher's hand, tried to speak but couldn't – and drifted out raining tears all over the place.

DISPATCH (diss <u>pach</u>) *v.* **-ing**, **-ed**
to send something or someone somewhere in a
hurry
Synonyms: transmit

Aunt Polly's happiness was complete, and Mrs. Thatcher's was nearly so. It would be complete, however, as soon as the messenger **dispatched** with the great news to the cave should get the word to her husband.

Tom lay upon a sofa and told the history of the wonderful adventure. He put in many striking additions to decorate it and closed with a description of how he left Becky and went on an exploring expedition. How he followed two avenues as far as his kite string would reach. How he followed a third to the fullest stretch of the kite string, and was about to turn back when he glimpsed a far-off speck that looked like daylight. How he dropped the string and groped toward the light, pushed his head and shoulders through a small hole, and saw the broad Mississippi rolling by! And if it had only happened to be night he would not have seen that speck of daylight and would not have explored that passage any more!

Tom told how he went back for Becky and broke the good news, and she told him not to fret her with such stuff, for she was tired and knew

LABOR (<u>lay</u> bur) *v.* **-ing**, **-ed**
to do hard work
Synonyms: toil, struggle

FAMISHED (<u>fam</u> isht) *adj.*
being very hungry
Synonyms: starving, ravenous

TOIL (toyl) *n.*
hard work
Synonyms: labor, effort, struggle

she was going to die and wanted to. He described how he **labored** with her and convinced her, and how she almost died for joy when she had groped to where she actually saw the blue dot of daylight. Then he told how he pushed his way out at the hole and then helped her out, how they sat there and cried for gladness. He then told how some men came along in a <u>skiff</u> and how he hailed them and told them the children's situation and their **famished** condition.

Tom went on about how the men in the skiff didn't believe the wild tale at first, "because," said they, "you are five miles down the river below the valley the cave is in." But then the men took them aboard, rowed to a house, gave them supper, made them rest till two or three hours after dark, and then brought them home.

Three days and nights of **toil** and hunger in the cave were not to be shaken off at once, as Tom and Becky soon discovered. They were <u>bedridden</u> all of Wednesday and Thursday and seemed to grow more and more tired and worn all the time. Tom got about, a little, on Thursday, was

IRONICALLY (eye <u>ron</u> ik lee) *adv.*
in a way that one expects to get an unusual result
Synonyms: mockingly, comically, humorously

PROSPECT (<u>pross</u> pekt) *n.*
something to look forward to or anticipate
Synonyms: expectation, hope

ABSENT (<u>ab</u> suhnt) *adj.*
not present
Synonyms: gone, missing, away

downtown Friday, and nearly as whole as ever Saturday. But Becky did not leave her room until Sunday, and then she looked as if she had passed through a wasting illness.

That day the Judge and some friends set Tom to talking, and some one asked him **ironically** if he wouldn't like to go to the cave again. Tom said he thought he wouldn't mind it. The judge said:

"Well, there are others just like you, Tom, I've not the least doubt. But we have taken care of that. Nobody will get lost in that cave any more."

"Why?"

"Because I'm going to put up a big door covered with iron, all triple-locked – and only I'll have the keys."

Tom turned as white as a sheet, as the **prospect** of retrieving his treasure seemed to disappear.

Tom decided to meet up with Huck to return to the cave before it was too late. So, just after noon the boys borrowed a small skiff from a citizen who was **absent** and got under way at once. They landed when they were several miles below "Cave Hollow."

CLUSTER (<u>kluhss</u> tur) *n.*
a bunch of things put or grown close together
Synonyms: group, collection

MARVELOUS (<u>mar</u> vuh luhss) *adj.*
outstanding or wonderful
Synonyms: spectacular, excellent, amazing

WAYLAY (<u>way</u> lay) *v.* **-ing**, **-ed**
to surprise or capture unexpectedly
Synonyms: ambush, intercept, rob

RANSOM (<u>ran</u> suhm) *n.*
money demanded to free a prisoner
Synonyms: payoff, settlement, price

"Now, Huck," said Tom, "where we're a-standing you could touch that hole I got out of with a fishing pole. See if you can find it."

Huck searched all the place about and found nothing. Tom proudly marched into a thick **cluster** of bushes and said:

"Here you are! Look at it, Huck. It's the snuggest hole in this country. You just keep <u>mum</u> about it. All along I've been wanting to be a robber, but I knew I'd got to have a thing like this, and where to run across it was the bother. We've got it now, and we'll keep it quiet, only we'll let Joe Harper and Ben Rogers in – because, of course, there's got to be a gang or else there wouldn't be any style about it. Tom Sawyer's Gang – it sounds **marvelous**, don't it, Huck?"

"Well, it just does, Tom. And who'll we rob?"

"Oh, most anybody. **Waylay** people – that's mostly the way."

"And kill them?"

"No, not always. Hide them in the cave till they raise a **ransom**."

EXPIRE (ek <u>spire</u>) *v.* **-ing**, **-ed**
to reach the end, to run out of time
Synonyms: finish, conclude, terminate

OPPRESS (uh <u>press</u>) *v.* **-ing**, **-ed**
to cause worry or weigh you down
Synonyms: demoralize, break

PRECIPICE (<u>press</u> uh piss) *n.*
a steep incline or a mass of rock
Synonyms: mountain, cliff

"Why, it's real <u>bully</u>, Tom. I believe it's better'n to be a pirate."

"Yes, it's better in some ways, because it's close to home and circuses and all that."

By this time everything was ready, and the boys entered the hole, Tom in the lead. They toiled their way to the farther end of the tunnel, then made their diverging kite-strings fast and moved on. A few steps brought them to the spring, and Tom felt a shudder go all the way through him. He showed Huck the piece of <u>candlewick</u> sitting on a lump of clay against the wall, and he described how he and Becky had watched the flame struggle and **expire**.

The boys began to quiet down to whispers, now, for the stillness and gloom of the place **oppressed** their spirits. They went on, and presently they entered and followed Tom's other corridor until they reached the "jumping-off place." The candles revealed the fact that it was not really a **precipice**, but only a clay hill twenty or thirty feet high.

"Now I'll show you something, Huck."

RECESS (<u>ree</u> sess) *n.*
a small hole or indentation
Synonyms: nook, niche, alcove

VAIN (vayn) *adj.*
futile or not successful
Synonyms: unsuccessful, useless

He held his candle aloft and said:

"Look as far around the corner as you can. Do you see that? There – on the big rock over yonder – done with candle-smoke."

"Tom, it's a CROSS!"

Tom went first, cutting rude steps in the clay hill as he descended. Huck followed. Four avenues opened out of the small cavern which the great rock stood in. The boys examined three of them with no result. They found a small **recess** in the one nearest the base of the rock, with blankets spread down in it. They also found an old suspender, some bacon, and the well-chewed bones of two or three chickens. But there was no money-box. The lads searched and researched this place, but in **vain**. Tom said:

"Do you think there's treasure UNDER the cross? If there is, it can't be under the rock itself, because that sets solid on the ground.

"Lookyhere, Huck, there's footprints and some candle-grease on the clay about one side of this rock, but not on the other sides. Now, what's that for? I bet your treasure IS under the rock. I'm going to dig in the clay."

ANIMATION (an uh <u>may</u> shun) *n.*
the condition of being lively and spirited
Synonyms: liveliness, vibrance, energy

CONCEAL (kuhn <u>seel</u>) *v.* **-ing**, **-ed**
to hide something
Synonyms: obscure, mask, cover

GRADUALLY (<u>graj</u> yoo-uhl ee) *adv.*
in a slow, careful manner
Synonyms: steadily, slowly

"That ain't no bad notion, Tom!" said Huck with **animation**.

Tom's shovel was out at once, and he had not dug four inches before he struck wood.

"Hey, Huck! – you hear that?"

Huck began to dig and scratch now. Some boards were soon uncovered and removed. They had **concealed** a natural chasm which led under the rock. Tom got into this and held his candle as far under the rock as he could, but he said he could not see to the end. He proposed to explore. He stooped and passed under. The narrow way descended **gradually**. He followed its winding course, first to the right, then to the left, Huck at his heels. Tom turned a short curve, by-and-by, and exclaimed:

"My goodness, Huck, lookyhere!"

It was the treasure-box, sure enough, occupying a snug little cavern, along with an empty powder keg, a couple of guns in leather cases, two or three pairs of old moccasins, a leather belt, and some other rubbish well soaked with the water-drip.

"Got it at last!" said Huck, sorting among the coins with his hand. "My, but we're rich, Tom!"

CONVENIENTLY (kuhn <u>vee</u> nyuhnt lee) *adv.*
in a comfortable, suitable way
Synonyms: easily, effortlessly

TRANSPORT (transs <u>port</u>) *v.* **-ing**, **-ed**
to move from one place to another
Synonyms: carry, transfer

It weighed about fifty pounds. Tom could lift it, but could not carry it **conveniently**. There were some bags buried too, which gave the boys something to **transport** the treasure in.

The money was soon in the bags, and the boys took it up to the cross rock. "Now less fetch the guns and things," said Huck.

"No, Huck – leave them there. They're just the tricks to have when we go to robbing. We'll keep them there all the time, and we'll hold our meetings there, too. It's an awful snug place for mischief."

They presently emerged into the clump of sumach bushes, looked carefully out, found the coast clear, and were soon lunching in the skiff.

"Now, Huck," said Tom, "we'll hide the money in the loft of my woodshed. I'll come up in the morning and we'll count it and divide it, and then we'll hunt up a place out in the woods for it where it will be safe."

He disappeared and presently returned with a wagon, put the two small sacks into it, threw some old rags on top of them, and started off, dragging his cargo behind him. Suddenly, the boys were

BECKON (<u>bek</u> uhn) *v.* **-ing, ed**
 to gesture someone over
  Synonyms: motion, wave

SUMMON (<u>sum</u> uhn) *v.* **-ing, -ed**
 to request someone to come, to send for
  Synonyms: send for, gather, assemble

HEARTILY (<u>hart</u> uh lee) *adv.*
 done with warmth and sincerity
  Synonyms: energetically, kindly

HUMILIATION (hyoo mil ee <u>ay</u> shun) *n.*
 the state of being embarrassed
  Synonyms: shame, disgrace

beckoned into Widow Douglas' house by Mr. Jones as they passed it by. A surprise awaited them as she **summoned** them into the house.

The place was grandly lighted, and everybody of any importance in the village was there. Old Widow Douglas received the boys as **heartily** as any one could well receive two beings covered with clay and candle-grease. Aunt Polly blushed <u>crimson</u> with **humiliation** and frowned and shook her head at Tom. Nobody suffered half as much as the two boys did, however. Mr. Jones said:

"Tom wasn't at home, yet, so I gave him up. But I stumbled on him and Huck right at the door, and so I just asked them in right away."

The widow took the boys to a bedchamber and said:

"Now wash and dress yourselves. Here are two new suits of clothes – shirts, socks, everything complete. They're Huck's – no, no thanks. But they'll fit both of you. Get into them. We'll wait – come down when you are dressed up enough."

Then she left.

ABSCOND (ab <u>skond</u>) *v.* **-ing**, **-ed**
to run away suddenly and secretly
Synonyms: escape, flee

CHAPTER 16

Huck said: "Tom, we can **abscond**, if we can find a rope. The window ain't high from the ground."

"Shucks! What do you want to run away for?"

"Well, I ain't used to that kind of a crowd. I can't stand it. I ain't going down there, Tom."

"Oh, bother! It ain't anything. I don't mind it a bit. I'll take care of you."

Sid appeared.

"Tom," said he, "auntie has been waiting for

ATTIRE (uh <u>tire</u>) *n.*
    things that are worn, clothes
        Synonym: outfit

CLANDESTINE (klan dess teen) *adj.*
    done out of public knowledge
        Synonyms: secret, furtive, concealed

INTENSE (in <u>tenss</u>) *adj.*
    very powerful and strong
        Synonyms: extreme, severe

you all the afternoon. Mary got your Sunday **attire** ready, and everybody's been worrying about you.

"Old Mr. Jones is going to try to spring something on the people here tonight. But I overheard him tell auntie today about it, as something **clandestine**, but I reckon it's not much of a secret now. Everybody knows – the widow, too, for all she tries to let on she don't."

Some minutes later the widow's guests were at the supper-table, and a dozen children were propped up at little side-tables in the same room, after the fashion of that country and that day.

The widow said she meant to give Huck a home under her roof and have him educated. Then, when she could spare the money, she would start him in business in a modest way. Tom's chance was come. He said:

"Huck don't need it. Huck's rich."

Nothing but an **intense** strain upon the good manners of the company kept back a laugh at this pleasant joke. But Tom wouldn't budge. "Huck's got money," he declared. "Maybe you don't believe it, but he's got lots of it. Oh, you needn't

PERPLEXED (pur <u>pleksd</u>) *adj.*
 suddenly puzzled or unsure
  Synonyms: confused, astonished, baffled

INQUIRINGLY (in <u>kwire</u> ing lee) *adv.*
 in a questioning way
  Synonyms: questioningly, pryingly

UNANIMOUS (yoo <u>nan</u> uh muhss lee) *adj.*
 without a negative vote or voice
  Synonyms: common, undisputed

TALLY (<u>tal</u> ee) *v.* **-ing**, **-ed**
 to count or factor
  Synonyms: compute, total

smile – I reckon I can show you. You just wait a minute."

Tom ran out of doors. The company looked at each other with a **perplexed** interest – and **inquiringly** at Huck, who was tongue-tied.

"Sid, what ails Tom?" said Aunt Polly. "He – well, there ain't ever any making of that boy out. I never—"

Tom entered, struggling with the weight of his sacks, and Aunt Polly did not finish her sentence. Tom poured the mass of yellow coin upon the table.

"There – what did I tell you? Half of it's Huck's, and half of it's mine!"

The spectacle took the general breath away. All gazed, nobody spoke for a moment. Then there was a **unanimous** call for an explanation, which Tom, of course, gladly gave. The tale was long, but full of interest. There was hardly an interruption from any one to break the charm of its flow. When Tom finished, the money was **tallied**. The sum amounted to a little over twelve thousand dollars. It was more than any one present had ever seen at one time before.

GLORIFY (<u>glor</u> if eye) *v.* **-ing**, **-ed**
to treat as important or splendid
Synonyms: praise, honor

DISSECT (di <u>sekt</u>) *v.* **-ing**, **-ed**
to analyze by taking apart
Synonyms: examine, divide, dismember

FOUNDATION (foun <u>day</u> shun) *n.*
a basis or bottom on which a building is
created
Synonyms: fundamental, support

CHAPTER 17

The reader may rest satisfied that Tom's and Huck's success made a mighty stir in the poor little village of St. Petersburg. Such a vast a sum, all in actual cash, seemed implausible to the poor villagers. It was talked about, bragged about, **glorified**, until the reason of many of the citizens left under the strain of the unhealthy excitement. Soon, the whole town was hunting for treasure. Every "haunted" house in St. Petersburg and the neighboring villages was **dissected**, plank by plank, and its **foundations** dug up and searched for hidden

PRODIGIOUS (pro <u>dij</u> uss) *adj.*
extremely large
Synonyms: huge, vast, extraordinary

MAGNANIMOUS (mag <u>nan</u> uh muhss) *adj.*
noble in heart and mind
Synonyms: generous, worthy, courageous

treasure – and not by boys, but men – pretty grave, serious-minded men, too, some of them. Wherever Tom and Huck appeared they were admired, stared at. The village paper published <u>biographical</u> sketches of the boys.

The Widow Douglas put Huck's money out at <u>six per cent</u>, and Judge Thatcher did the same with Tom's. Each lad had an income, now, that was simply **prodigious** – a dollar for every weekday in the year and half of the Sundays. A dollar and a quarter a week would board, lodge, and school a boy in those old simple days – and clothe him and wash him, too, for that matter.

Judge Thatcher had developed a great opinion of Tom. He said that no commonplace boy would ever have got his daughter out of the cave. When Becky told her father how Tom had taken her whipping at school, the Judge was visibly moved. And when she pleaded grace for the mighty lie which Tom had told in order to shift that whipping from her shoulders to his own, the Judge said with a fine outburst that it was a noble, a generous, a **magnanimous** lie. Becky thought her father had

SUPERB (su <u>purb</u>) *adj.*
of unusually high quality
Synonyms: terrific, fabulous, wonderful

PERUSE (pur <u>ooz</u>) *v.* **-ing**, **-ed**
to read in a thorough manner
Synonym: examine

INSIPID (in <u>sip</u> id) *adj.*
lacking in flavor or excitement
Synonyms: dull, unexciting, boring

TOLERATE (<u>tol</u> uh rate) *v.* **-ing**, **-ed**
to endure or put up with something
Synonyms: bear, accept, endure

never looked so tall and so **superb** as when he walked the floor and stamped his foot and said that. She went straight off and told Tom about it.

Huck Finn's wealth and the fact that he was now under the Widow Douglas' protection introduced him into society – no, dragged him into it, hurled him into it – and his sufferings were almost more than he could bear. The widow's servants kept him clean and neat, combed and brushed, and they bedded him nightly in clean sheets that had not one little spot or stain which he could press to his heart and know for a friend. He had to eat with a knife and fork. He had to **peruse** his book, and he had to go to church. He had to talk so properly that speech became **insipid** in his mouth. Wherever he turned, the bars and chains of civilization shut him in and bound him hand and foot.

He bravely **tolerated** his miseries three weeks, and then one day he turned up missing. For forty-eight hours the widow hunted for him everywhere in great distress. The townspeople were profoundly concerned. They searched high and low, and they dragged the river for his body.

REFUGEE (<u>ref</u> yoo jee) *n.*
someone forced to leave his or her home
Synonyms: escapee, deserter, fugitive

UNKEMPT (un <u>kemt</u>) *adj.*
not properly maintained or kept in an orderly
manner
Synonyms: untidy, disorderly, uncombed

TRANQUIL (<u>trang</u> kwuhl) *adj.*
free from disturbance or anxiety
Synonyms: calm, restful, quiet, peaceful

SMOTHER (<u>smuth</u> ur) *v.* **-ing**, **-ed**
to take away air, freedom, or movement
Synonyms: suffocate, choke, stifle

Early the third morning Tom Sawyer wisely went poking among some old empty barrels down behind the abandoned slaughterhouse, and in one of them he found the **refugee**. He had just breakfasted upon some stolen odds and ends of food, and he was lying, now, in comfort, smoking his pipe. He was **unkempt** and clad in the same old ruin of rags that had made him so unusual in the days when he was free and happy. Tom got him out, told him the trouble he had been causing, and urged him to go home. Huck's face lost its **tranquil** content, and took a melancholy cast. He said:

"Don't talk about it, Tom. I've tried it, and it don't work. It don't work, Tom. The widder's good to me and friendly. But I can't stand them ways. She makes me get up just at the same time every morning. She makes me wash, and they comb me all to thunder. She won't let me sleep in the woodshed. I got to wear them blamed clothes that just **smothers** me, Tom. I got to go to church, and I hate them <u>ornery</u> sermons! The widder eats by a bell, she goes to bed by a bell, and she gits up by a bell – everything's so awful reg'lar a body can't stand it."

SPASM (<u>spaz</u> uhm) *n.*
a small, sudden burst of activity or energy
Synonyms: tremor, contraction, shudder

IRRITATION (ihr uh <u>tay</u> shun) *n.*
something that bothers or annoys
Synonyms: nuisance, exasperation

"Well, everybody does that way, Huck."

"Tom, it don't make a difference. I ain't everybody, and I can't STAND it. And <u>grub</u> comes too easy – I don't take no interest in little things, that way. I got to ask to go fishing. I got to ask to go in swimming. Dern'd if I hain't got to ask to do everything. The widder wouldn't let me smoke. She wouldn't let me yell. She wouldn't let me stretch nor scratch in front of folks."

Then with a **spasm** of special **irritation** and injury, Huck declared, "And what's worse, she prayed all the time! I never seen such a woman! I HAD to shove off, Tom – I just had to. And besides, that school's going to open, and I'd a had to go to it – well, I wouldn't stand THAT, Tom. Looky here, Tom, being rich ain't what it's cracked up to be. It's just worry and worry, and sweat and sweat. Tom, I wouldn't ever got into all this trouble if it hadn't 'a' ben for that money. Now you just take my share of it along with your'n, and gimme a ten-cent piece sometimes – not many times, becuz I don't give a dern for a thing 'thout it's tolerable hard

DURATION (dur <u>ay</u> shun) *n.*
a measure or amount of time
Synonyms: period, phase, episode

EARNEST (<u>ur</u> nist) *adj.*
showing sincerity or truthfulness
Synonyms: intense, serious

to git – and you go and beg off for me with the widder."

"Oh, Huck, you know I can't do that. 'Tain't fair. And besides if you'll try this thing just a while longer you'll come to like it."

"Like it! Yes – the way I'd like a hot stove if I was to set on it for a long enough **duration**. No, Tom, I won't be rich, and I won't live in them cussed smothery houses. I like the woods, and the river, and barrels, and I'll stick to 'em, too. Blame it all! Just as we'd got guns and a cave and all just fixed to rob, here this dern foolishness has got to come up and spoil it all!"

Tom saw his opportunity –

"Lookyhere, Huck, being rich ain't going to keep me back from turning robber."

"No! Oh, are you real **earnest** about that?

"Just as dead earnest as I'm sitting here. But Huck, we can't let you into the gang if you ain't respectable, you know."

Huck's joy was quenched.

"Can't let me in, Tom? Didn't you let me go for a pirate?"

NOBILITY (noh <u>bil</u> eh tee) *n.*
people of high status or morality
Synonyms: aristocracy

ATTEMPT (uh <u>tempt</u>) *v.* **-ing, -ed**
to try to do
Synonyms: try, endeavor, venture

"Yes, but that's different. A robber is more high-toned than what a pirate is – as a general thing. In most countries they're awful high up in the **nobility** – dukes and such."

"Now, Tom, hain't you always been friendly to me? You wouldn't shut me out, would you, Tom? You wouldn't do that now, WOULD you, Tom?"

"Huck, I wouldn't want to, and I DON'T want to. But what would people say? Why, they'd say, 'Mph! Tom Sawyer's Gang! Pretty low characters in it!' They'd mean you, Huck. You wouldn't like that, and I wouldn't."

Huck was silent for some time, engaged in a mental struggle. Finally he said:

"Well, I'll go back to the widder for a month and **attempt** it and see if I can come to stand it, if you'll let me b'long to the gang, Tom."

"All right, Huck, it's a deal! Come along, old chap, and I'll ask the widow to let up on you a little, Huck."

"Will you, Tom – now will you? That's good. If she'll let up on some of the roughest things, I'll smoke private and cuss private, and make it

INITIATION (uh nish ee <u>ay</u> shun) *n.*
a ritual that allows someone to enter a group
Synonym: ceremony

EXHILARATING (eks <u>il</u> ur ay ting) *adj.*
causing excitement
Synonyms: thrilling, uplifting

through or bust. When you going to start the gang and turn robbers?"

"Oh, right off. We'll get the boys together and have the **initiation** tonight, maybe."

"Have the which?"

"Have the initiation."

"What's that?"

"It's to swear to stand by one another and never tell the gang's secrets, even if you're chopped all to bits, and to kill anybody and all his family that hurts one of the gang."

"That's nice – that's mighty nice, Tom.

"Well, I bet it is. And all that swearing's got to be done at midnight, in the lonesomest, awfulest place you can find."

"Well, midnight's good, anyway, Tom."

"Yes, so it is. And you've got to swear on a coffin and sign it with blood."

"Now, that's something I like! Why, it's a million times more **exhilarating** than pirating. I'll stick to the widder, Tom. And if I git to be a reg'lar robber, and everybody talking 'bout it, I reckon she'll be proud she snaked me in out of the wet."

CHRONICLE (<u>kron</u> ik uhl) *n.*
 a long piece of writing that tells a story
 Synonyms: account, narrative, story

PROSPEROUS (<u>pros</u> pur uss) *adj.*
 having money and position in society
 Synonyms: wealthy, successful

CONCLUSION

So endeth this **chronicle**. It being strictly a history of a BOY, it must stop here. The story could not go much further without becoming the history of a MAN. When one writes a novel about grown people, he knows exactly where to stop – that is, with a marriage. But when he writes of juveniles, he must stop where he best can.

Most of the characters in this book still live and are **prosperous** and happy. Some day it may seem worth while to take up the story of the younger ones again and see what sort of men and women they turned out to be. Therefore it will be wisest not to reveal any of that part of their lives at present.

RESOURCES

GLOSSARY

The following are words and terms that you are not likely to be tested on, but understanding them may enhance your appreciation of the text.

aide (ayd) *n.*
a person who helps another person work

anatomy (uh <u>nat</u> uh mee) *n.*
the study of the physical structure of living things, the study of the bodies of creatures

bedridden (<u>bed</u> rid uhn) *adj.*
unable to get out of bed, usually because of illness

biographical (bye uh <u>graf</u> uh kuhl) *adj.*
relating to someone's biography or life story

bully (bul ee) *adj.*
slang word meaning "hooray" popular during the 1800s and early 1900s

bygone (<u>bye</u> gon) *adj.*
past

candlewick (<u>kan</u> duhl wick) *n.*
the piece of string in the middle of a candle

crimson (<u>krim</u> zuhn) *n.*
a deep red color

crystal (<u>kriss</u> tuhl) *n.*
a clear mineral or rock

departed (di <u>part</u> ed) *n.*
those who have died or gone away

druther (<u>druhth</u> uhr) *adv.*
rather

engaged (en <u>gayjd</u>) *adj.* **-ing, -ed**
ready to get married

fry (frye) *n.*
little ones, like children

geography (jee <u>og</u> ruh fee) *n.*
the study of the earth

giddy (<u>gid</u> ee) *adj.*
unsteady, dizzy

grub (grub) *n.*
food

harp (harp) *n.*
a musical instrument that makes sounds from
pulling on strings

harum-scarum (<u>hair</u> uhm <u>scair</u> uhm) *adj.*
reckless, irresponsible

hoarse (horss) *adj.*
to have a rough, sore throat

hooky (<u>hook</u> ee) *n.*
staying out of school without permission

ice house *n.*
a place where ice is made or stored; in the days
before electric refrigerators, ice houses were a
common way of storing food

lick (lick) *v.* **-ing**, **-ed**
to beat up

Mont Blanc (mahnt blahnk) *n.*
mountain in the Alps; during the 1800s it was a
popular destination for mountain climbers

mope (mope) *v.* **-ing**, **-ed**
to move in a sad, downcast way

mum (muhm) *adj.*
quiet, silent

ornery (<u>or</u> nur ee) *adj.*
stubborn and mean

played out (playd <u>out</u>) *v.*
finished, exhausted

p'raps (prapps) *adv.*
perhaps, maybe

sass (sas) *n.*
   disrespectful or insulting speech

score (skore) *n.*
   twenty of something

six per cent *adj.*
   an interest, or charge, at the rate of 6 per 100

skiff (skif) *n.*
   a small boat, usually moved by rowing oars

slate (slayt) *n.*
   a blue-gray rock; during the 1800s
   schoolchildren wrote on thin pieces of slate
   with chalk

steamboat (<u>steem</u> boht) *n.*
   a boat powered by a steam engine; during the
   1800s, steamboats carried goods up and down
   the Mississippi River

straightaway (<u>strayt</u> uh way) *adv.*
Without a delay, immediately

sumach (<u>soo</u> mak) *n.*
a bush or tree with pointed leaves and clusters
of flowers or berries

tease (teez) *v.* **-ing**, **-ed**
to nag or pester

thrashing (<u>thrash</u> ing) *n.*
a beating

toll (tohl) *v.* **-ing**, **-ed**
to ring a bell very solemnly and slowly

urchin (<u>uhr</u> chin) *n.*
a child

wick (wick) *n.*
candlewick, the string in the middle of a candle

BOOK REPORT

The key to writing a good report is to organize your ideas before you start writing. Use the following questions to organize your ideas for a book report about *Tom Sawyer*

1. What is the title?
2. Who is the author? What do you know about the author and his life?
3. When and where does the story take place?
4. Who are the main characters of the book?
5. What happens to these people during the story? What are these people like at the beginning? And at the end? What problems do these people face? How do these people solve those problems?
6. What does the book tell you about life at the time the novel takes place?
7. What do you think is the main theme or idea of the book?
8. What is the main thing you learned from this book?
9. What would you tell a friend about this book if he or she asked you about it?

DISCUSSION QUESTIONS

Here are several questions to think about and to discuss with classmates, friends, and other people who have read Mark Twain's *Tom Sawyer.*

1. Tom often dreams of leading a life of adventure as a pirate, a robber, or some other kind of outlaw. Why do you think these roles appeal to Tom?

2. For many years, readers have thought of Tom as the kind of young person they themselves would like to be. Why do you think Tom appeals to readers in this way?

3. How does Aunt Polly feel about Tom? How does he feel about her?

4. Why do you think the town's children are so interested in Huck Finn?

5. What do you think will happen to Tom in the future? What kind of teenager and adult do you think he will be?